"Ohh, Hobie! You Wrote a Poem for Me!"

"NO!" This was the worst—more than any normal guy could be expected to live through.

I lunged for G. G. "No, I didn't. Give me that!"

She held it away from me. "No, it's beautiful. I want to keep it."

I grabbed the poem. She backed away, looking confused. "But, Hobie, it's good. I never knew you—"

"It's not for you!" Darlene was staring at us, fascinated, her violet eyes fixed on my red, bulging ones.

I glanced at the poem. It was the good one, the almost perfect one.

I grabbed all my books, and before I could stop myself, as if I was being driven by some mysterious unknown force, I lurched toward Darlene.

"It's for *you*," I said hoarsely, and dropped it on the table in front of her.

Books by Ellen Conford

AND THIS IS LAURA
ANYTHING FOR A FRIEND
FELICIA THE CRITIC
HAIL, HAIL CAMP TIMBERWOOD
LENNY KANDELL, SMART ALECK
THE LUCK OF POKEY BLOOM
ME AND THE TERRIBLE TWO

WHY ME?

Available from ARCHWAY Paperbacks

Ellen Conford

Why Me?

AN ARCHWAY PAPERBACK
Published by POCKET BOOKS • NEW YORK

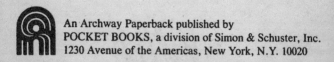

An Archway Paperback published by
POCKET BOOKS, a division of Simon & Schuster, Inc.
1230 Avenue of the Americas, New York, N.Y. 10020

Published by arrangement with Little, Brown and Company, Inc.
Library of Congress Catalog Card Number: 85-214

ISBN: 0-671-62841-0

First Archway Paperback printing February 1987

10 9 8 7 6 5 4 3 2 1

AN ARCHWAY PAPERBACK and colophon are
registered trademarks of Simon & Schuster, Inc.

Printed in the U.S.A.

❧ 1 ❧

I WAS JUST STANDING THERE, MINDING MY OWN business, when G. G. Graffman wheeled her bike right into Bookathon and ruined my life.

"You can't bring that bike in here, G. G.," I said. "You have to leave it outside."

She stood there stubbornly holding onto the seat, her Orphan Annie hair looking as if it would burst into flame at any moment. "I can't leave it outside; it'll get stolen."

"Lock it on the bike rack."

"I can't. Somebody stole my lock."

"Somebody stole your lock and left your bike?" I asked incredulously.

"Look, Hobie, it's taking longer to argue about this than it would for me to buy my book. Your grandfather won't mind."

"All right, all right, but hurry up. You're blocking the whole magazine rack."

G. G. nudged the kickstand down with her foot

1

and sprinted past the Flaming Desire romances. In her gray warm-up jacket and pants she looked exactly the same from the back as she did from the front, except her toes were pointing the wrong way.

It was five o'clock. Even though the rest of the Million Dollar Mall was still humming there wasn't anyone else in my grandfather's store, so I supposed it didn't matter about the bike. I shrugged, forgot about G. G., and went back to reading the newest Mac Detroit book.

It was really good. It was called *Terminate with Extreme Pain*, and I was just at the spot where the beautiful Eurasian girl skulks into Mac's hotel room with a dagger in her teeth when . . .

"Hobie? Can I pay for this now?"

I looked up, startled, almost expecting to see the girl in the slinky black satin dress, but it was only G. G., gazing at me with her big green eyes.

She had nice eyes, I had to admit that. But that was about it, appeal-wise.

She held up the back of the book. "Don't look at the title, okay?"

"How can I tell how much it costs if I don't look at the cover?"

"The price is on the back too. See, right down there. Five ninety-five."

"I've got news for you, G. G. The title's on the back too."

"Oh." She dropped the book on the counter and made a big show of searching her jacket pocket for money.

2

WHY ME?

Now, we bookstore people are trained never to bat an eyelash or make a comment on the books our customers buy unless it's a perfectly ordinary purchase like a cookbook or the latest best-seller, something like that. I mean, I'd worked in my grandfather's store for a year and I've seen people buy books you wouldn't believe.

There was the sweet little old lady who bought a copy of *The Art of Sensual Massage* and the hulking fullback type who had me ring up *Jane Fonda's Workout Book*. Then there was the mother with the screaming three-year-old twins who bought *Killer Karate from A to Z*. Come to think of it, maybe that last one wasn't such a bizarre choice.

Anyhow, you get the idea. I never make a comment, never embarrass the customer, just take the money or write up the charge slip; that's it.

Which is what I did with G. G.'s book. Even though it was called *How to Make Men Crazy* and I wanted to fall down laughing on the floor.

Mr. Cool. Take the six dollars and ten cents, slip the book in a green Bookathon bag, throw in the free bookmark.

"Thank you very much. Have a nice day."

"Do you *mean* it, Hobie?"

"Mean what? Have a nice day? Sure I mean it. Even though it's evening already."

"You say that to everybody."

"Everybody says that to everybody, G. G. I was just being polite."

"That's what I thought." She seemed a little dejected. "Well, see you."

3

She wheeled the bike out, holding the green bag in her teeth, and I went back to Mac Detroit.

Only I couldn't concentrate.

The last book in the world you'd expect G. G. Graffman to buy was *How to Make Men Crazy.* The girl was born with a microscope in her hand; her first words were "marine biology," and her idea of dressing up was to tie the laces on her Nikes. Every time she came to the store she bought stuff like *Plankton: Mysterious Denizen of the Deep,* or *Analyze Seawater in Your Own Back Yard.* For light reading I figured she relaxed with *Killer Shrimp from Outer Space.*

Once she came in and asked if we had anything new in her field and I suggested *Venus on the Half Shell* by Kilgore Trout. She looked at me kind of blankly for a minute, then said, "No, I'm not into clam mythology."

The girl is bright, but she has no sense of humor.

Anyway, the last thing you'd expect G. G. to have on her mind was driving men crazy. Now, Darlene DeVries—she's another kettle of fish.

Darlene DeVries didn't need a book to tell her how to drive men crazy. Darlene could have written the book. She didn't come into the store too often, but she was in my English class in school, and she drove me crazy for forty-two minutes every day.

She sat two desks in front of me and had this habit of tossing her long, silky-blonde hair back and hitting my friend, Nate, in the face with it. This drove *Nate* crazy, because he kept getting her hair

4

in his eyes and mouth, along with, as he said, "God knows what else."

I said I'd change places with him in a minute, so the next day we did, but Mr. Schulman made me take my assigned seat, and I never did get to feel Darlene's hair sweep across my face.

I looked at my watch. It was five forty-five. In fifteen minutes, Jennifer, a college student, would take over and my grandfather would drive me home, have dinner, and go back to the store. I couldn't believe I'd been thinking about G. G. for half an hour. (With maybe five minutes for Darlene, which just goes to show you how an unexpected event can mess up your priorities.)

What had G. G. meant when she asked, "Do you mean it?"? Who means it when he says, "Have a nice day"? And why did she look so disappointed when I said I was just being polite? I couldn't concentrate on Mac Detroit and the beautiful Eurasian assassin. G. G. was driving me nuts.

Aha! *How to Make Men Crazy* was working already. She'd only bought it half an hour ago, and already G. G. was driving one man crazy: namely me.

Then I think I turned pale. I may even have clutched at my throat but I can't swear to it.

Was it possible, I wondered, as my sweat glands shifted into overdrive, that G. G. was out to make *me* crazy? Why else the weird question about my sincerity? If she wasn't about to hit on me, why should she care if my "Have a nice day" was heartfelt or prerecorded?

I never would have thought you could be flattered and nauseous at the same time. Until that moment.

"Oh, I don't know," Nate said. "She's not so bad. I mean, nothing to get sick over."

It was Saturday evening and we were at my house waiting for Pizza on Parade to deliver two extra-cheese specials.

"I didn't mean really sick," I said. "It's just— well, you know. Me and the Empress of Algae? What did I ever do to interest G. G.? Assuming she's interested, God forbid."

"Beats me," Nate said. "But what would Darlene DeVries want with you either?"

"She could use me as a scatter rug," I said fervently. "A lapdog, a bookend, whatever—I don't care—anything she wants."

"Look at this, sports fans!" Nate said in his announcer voice. "I think—I think—YES! A little bit of drool is trickling down the corner of his lip, a look of intense longing is coming into his eye—"

"Oh, shut up, Nate," I said impatiently. "What am I going to do?"

"Hobe, let me break this to you gently. You don't have to do anything, because nothing's happened yet. Did G. G. get herself gift-wrapped and delivered to your house? Did she attack you in the store? Did she Krazy-Glue herself to you in Social Studies? No, right? If you were a lobster—well, that would be another kettle of fish. Ho ho."

"Ho ho," I said sourly. "Dire things are about to happen to me, Nate. I can feel it. That girl is after me, she's studying how to make men crazy, and I'm going to be her first victim."

"Even if you're right," Nate said, "and I'm not for one minute agreeing with you, there *is* one last tiny shred of comfort you can cling to."

"What's that?"

"She's a *very* good student."

2

Sometimes my father gets impatient with me.

Occasionally I can sort of see his mood in perspective, because at times my grandfather gets very impatient with my father, especially when my father gets impatient with me.

But my grandfather isn't around all the time and my father is, and I've found that on an average of three days a week I can be sure I'm going to disappoint him. Somehow.

Usually it's because I have no "goals." At least, no long-term goals, as my father puts it. (I had short-term goals, mostly involving Darlene, but I didn't think they would interest my father. My grandfather, maybe.)

Ever since I turned fourteen, my father has been asking me what I want to do with my life.

How do I know? My father wants me to start thinking about choosing a college. Right now I'd like to make it through ninth grade.

My father says, "But don't you want to be *anything?* Haven't you any *idea* about a career?" My grandfather argues with him, my mother argues with him, but it never does any good. I used to keep telling him I was still a kid, and he'd say, "Sure, you're a kid when it's convenient, but when you want something you're practically all grown up."

This seemed irrelevant to me, but I finally figured out that the only way to deal with the pressure was to say something—anything—when he gave me the third degree. Like, for instance, "Oh, yeah, I decided I want to be a computer programmer."

A couple of days later he'd ask if I checked out the computer facilities at school, or if I'd looked through any college catalogues, and I'd say, "Yeah. I don't think that's for me. I'm not that good in math anyway. I'm thinking about law."

It holds him off for a while, and at least makes him think I'm taking my future as seriously as he does, which I guess is all he wants. My grandfather caught on pretty quickly to what I was doing, but my grandfather's pretty shrewd, and he sees me almost as much as my parents do.

The Bookathon store is what Grandpa calls his "Dream," and what my father calls his "crazy fantasy." He used to be an investment analyst. I guess he wasn't a very good one, because he and Grandma were never rich. When he retired he took most of the money he saved up and bought the bookstore. He owns it, but it's part of a big chain, so it's not exactly the bookstore of his dreams, which would be cozy and old-fashioned and not in the Million Dollar Mall. But he says you have to go with the times.

He hired me to help him last year because he said I was mature for my age and responsible—he said that right in front of my father, who doesn't share his opinion—and because he can pay me below the minimum wage. I don't know if he really meant that last part, but I needed the money and Grandpa knew I did.

Once, when my father was pestering me, I said, "Maybe I'll own a bookstore, like Grandpa's," and I thought he would turn purple. He was practically on the phone, ready to scream, "See what kind of an influence you are?" to his father when I said, "Joke, Dad. Just my little joke. I know there's no money in bookstores."

"That kind of joke," my mother said, "can cause cardiac arrest."

I decided what I wanted to be when I was twelve and started reading the Mac Detroit books. I wanted to be Mac Detroit—quick on the trigger, fast with the women, living hard and playing hard, facing death and danger at every corner, prowling the seamy underbelly of society in search of killers, thugs, secret agents, and dope smugglers.

At first I was more interested in the bullets Mac was dodging than the women he wasn't, but when I turned thirteen, I found the guns and the girls equally engrossing.

I realized that Mac Detroit was an adolescent fantasy written by a man named Mike Spain, who probably wouldn't know the difference between an

international vice ring and the Kiwanis Club. I
understood that wanting to become another Mac
Detroit was *my* adolescent fantasy. But my father is
very big on what he calls "role models," and when
he pressed me to pick out someone I admired and
strive to be like that person, I always thought of
Mac Detroit.

This is not something I can tell my father, who
owns an insurance agency and who, when he talks
about "role models," really means "Why can't you
be like me?"

I admire my father—within reason. He works out
at a gym twice a week and is in great condition. He
bought me all the equipment I wanted to start
weight training, and taught me how to do lifts and
curls and bench presses. He planned a whole body-
building program for me.

But I don't want to be like him. Even though he's
in better shape than Mac Detroit.

When the pizzas arrived that Saturday evening
and we were all sitting at the kitchen table dividing
them up, my father started in on Nate.

"So, Nate, I suppose you've begun to make
college plans."

Nate was eyeing the pizzas the way I looked at
Darlene. "I guess you could say that." I knew he
was dying to sink his teeth into meatballs, onions,
and cheese, but he restrained himself. "My plan is
not to go."

"Not go to college?" My mother looked surprised.

"What kind of career can you have without a degree?" my father asked.

Nate fought with a twelve-inch strand of cheese. "I'm going to be a sportscaster. You know, like Marv Albert."

My father seemed at a loss for words. But only for a moment.

"Is that—um—a very realistic possibility? Career-wise?"

"Gee, I don't know, Mr. Katz. But that's what I want to be."

My father chewed silently for a while, then said, "Well, at least you know your own mind."

My mother sighed. "Roger, don't start."

"I know what I want to be," I said firmly. "I've made up my mind. A marine biologist." I don't know why I said that. I guess talking about G. G. before the pizzas came had given me the idea.

Nate began to choke on his pizza. His face was bright red and I knew he was just laughing and trying not to spit meatballs and onions over everything, but my parents were pretty alarmed.

"It's okay," he gasped. "I think an anchovy got stuck in my throat."

My mother frowned. "I specifically told them no anchovies."

"I guess one must've swum in by mistake."

"A marine biologist." My father had this sort of hopeful look in his eyes. I really surprised him with that one. Myself, too.

"Have you—"

"Most of the top schools are in California," I said. I guess G. G. must have told me that once.

"California!" My mother didn't seem pleased at all.

Suddenly it was as if my father snapped back to reality.

"Don't worry about it, Elaine. Next week he'll change his mind again."

Nate jabbed me in the ribs. "By next week," he whispered, "a marine biologist may be studying *you*. Stay tuned, sports fans."

After the pizzas my mother drove Nate and me to the mall so we could go to the movies. They have this big theater called The Million Dollar Multiplex and they show twelve separate movies, so there's always something to see.

There was a really long line in front of the ticket window. We had plenty of time to decide which theater to go to.

"Fiery Fists of Death or *The Young Cutthroats,"* Nate said. "A tough decision."

"The Young Cutthroats is rated 'R,' " I pointed out. "They won't let us in."

"You don't think we can pass for seventeen?"

"We never have yet. There are ten other movies to choose from, Nate."

"Not when you got a Disney, a ballet movie, a doctor movie, a—holy cow, sports fans, look who's coming our way and ready to play."

"Who? Where?" I demanded.

"Here she comes, bringing the ball up court, flanked by her two teammates. She moves right to avoid a stroller, she moves left to avoid a trash can—"

It was Darlene DeVries.

"Boy, I'd like to hear what my colleague in the booth thinks about this development. Whaddya say, Horrible Hobe?"

"Shut up, will you? Just cool out."

"You heard it here first, fans, Horrible Hobie's incisive analysis. And another first, viewers. This is the first time in my long and distinguished broadcasting career that I've seen a sports announcer fall hopelessly in love with one of the players."

"Stop it!" My voice sounded like I was strangling. For a minute I thought I'd swallowed my tongue.

"Hi, Hobie," Darlene said, as she got behind us on line. "Going to the movies?"

Let me be the first to admit, here and now, that Darlene DeVries is not one of your world-class intellects. Let me also admit that I didn't care if her I.Q. was in single digits.

Her friends, Lesley Parker and Shawna Shepherd, stood on either side of her.

Nate turned around. "Actually, we're here for the Harvest Prune Festival. They pick a Miss Prune and everything. Aren't you one of the contestants?"

Darlene giggled.

"No, I guess you're not wrinkled enough. Wrin-

14

kles are one of the major requirements for Miss Prune. Along with the talent competition."

Darlene giggled again, although Shawna and Lesley ignored Nate.

"Cut it out," I said under my breath. "Stop making her laugh."

"You want me to make her cry?"

"I just want—"

"What movie are you going to see?" Darlene asked us. Shawna and Lesley looked bored.

"We can't decide between—" Nate began.

"What movie are *you* going to see?" I cut in.

"Toujours Jeté," Darlene said. That was the ballet movie.

"What a coincidence! So are we."

Nate yelped, like he was in pain. He grabbed my arm and pulled me forward as the line inched toward the ticket window. "Are you crazy? I'm not going to see any *ballet* movie. I wouldn't be caught dead—"

"Forget the movie," I said, out of the corner of my mouth. "We can sit next to them. I'll take Darlene and you can have Shawna and Lesley."

"I don't want Shawna and Lesley!" Nate exploded.

"Keep your voice down!"

But it really wasn't necessary, because behind us the three girls began to giggle and talk in loud, chirpy voices like they were trying to make people notice them.

I glanced over my shoulder and saw that Warren

15

Adler and two of his obscenely tall basketball team-mates had just gotten into line behind the three girls.

Obviously the girls were showing off for Warren and his friends, and I began to get a little tense. Warren was a junior, and Darlene only a ninth-grader, and although a school superstar might not be interested in a fourteen-year-old under ordinary circumstances, Darlene was no ordinary fourteen-year-old.

On the other hand, it was unlikely that Warren would spend cash money to see *Toujours Jeté*, no matter how many times he'd heard that ballet was just as athletic as any sport. I might still have a chance to sit with Darlene, who, under ordinary circumstances, would probably never sit with me if there was a chance she could sit next to Warren Adler.

By this time we were finally at the ticket window.

"Two for *Fiery Fists of Death*," Nate said.

"Two for *Toujours Jeté*," I said at the same time.

"You want four tickets?" the woman asked.

"No, just two," said Nate. *"Fiery Fists of Death."*

"Toujours Jeté." I whispered. I wasn't crazy about anyone knowing I was going to a ballet movie either, and any minute now people would start wondering who was holding up the line.

"Make up your mind," the woman said. "Which is it?"

Drastic times call for drastic measures. Mac De-troit wouldn't have thought twice about it and neither did I. There was a brief scuffle as I grabbed Nate's neck in a hammerlock and clamped my hand over his mouth. "I'm paying," I said, "so it's *Toujours Jeté*."

She punched out two tickets to Theater Six. Nate threatened to punch me out. I paid for the tickets and walked extremely slowly toward the ticket taker. I was waiting for Darlene to catch up with us.

Darlene and her friends were walking extremely slowly also, until Warren Adler and his cronies had paid for their tickets.

Nate was rubbing his neck and making death threats. I paid no attention.

The candy counter was swarming with kids. Nate indicated by a low snarl that he wanted popcorn, which was okay with me, because Darlene, Shawna, and Lesley decided to buy popcorn too, after the basketball players got on the popcorn line.

At last all eight of us had popcorn. I followed Darlene toward Theater Six. Darlene followed Warren, and for one awful moment I thought she had doublecrossed me and decided to go to whatever movie Warren was going to, but Warren and his friends went into Theater Five, where *Fiery Fists of Death* was playing, and Lesley just giggled, "See you later," as the team disappeared.

Darlene kept moving.

"Follow her," I whispered. Nate was hurling popcorn into his mouth with wild and reckless swoops of his arm.

"I'm going to rip your throat out," he said, popcorn spurting between his lips.

The audience for the ballet movie was pretty thin, which didn't surprise me, so I knew we could be near Darlene and her friends wherever they sat.

I lingered by the door with Nate, watching them debate over seats, ready to move down the aisle the minute they agreed.

Nate scarfed down popcorn and made plans to barbecue my liver for his dog.

"There they go," I said. "Down there. Let's move."

I gave him a little shove, and he started clumping down the aisle, leaving a trail of popcorn that crunched under my sneakers.

The lights went down and we slipped into the row behind Darlene. The movie started with a shot of a toe shoe twirling in a blue mist, with the "Blue Danube" waltz playing in the background.

Nate punched me in the biceps.

"OW!"

Darlene, Shawna, and Lesley turned around.

"Oh, hi, Hobie," Darlene said.

"Hi there." I tried to sound as if I wasn't writhing in pain. "Fancy meeting you here."

Darlene giggled. Lesley and Shawna turned back to the screen.

"Hi, Nate," Darlene said.

Nate growled.

Ten minutes into the movie, Shawna scampered up the aisle. A few minutes later she trotted back and sat down. The three girls held a whispered conference; the only thing I could make out sounded like "No one's there now."

A minute later Darlene, Lesley, and Shawna slipped out of their seats and headed back up the aisle.

"Probably getting more candy," I told Nate. "They'll be right back." I hoped I was right—but I had a funny feeling the girls were not going to get candy. They still had their popcorn boxes. And they'd taken their jackets.

Ten more minutes went by. It seemed longer, but that may have been because of all the ballet I was sitting through.

"They're not coming back," I said finally, defeated. "They must have sneaked into Five."

Nate turned my way for the first time and looked directly at me, his eyes glittering in the dark. "You mean, I am sitting here watching fairy princesses hop around on their toes *for no reason at all?* Is that what you're trying to tell me?"

"If they could sneak into the other theater, we probably could too. Come on."

Nate actually smiled.

First we walked all the way around the twelve theaters to the bathroom, where we hung out for a couple of minutes. This was so no one would see us walk right out of Six and into Five. That didn't seem very likely, because the only usher around was flirting with the girl at the candy counter, but there was no point in taking chances.

"Look nonchalant," I advised, as we strolled out of the men's room and past theaters Twelve through Seven. Nate nodded and tried to whistle. No sound came out, but a lot of popcorn did.

19

There was no usher outside Theater Five, so we eased the door open and slid in. Theater Five was mobbed, and no wonder. On the screen two Oriental guys were trying to tap-dance on each other's teeth, and the grunts, screams, and general sound effects were terrific. Everybody was yelling and cheering.

"Oh boy!" said Nate. "Oh boy!"

I just had time to wonder how come they didn't call the movie *Fiery* Feet *of Death* when an usher in a red jacket, who had cunningly concealed himself in a little niche between the last row of seats and the door, stepped between us.

"Out!"

"Hey, wait a minute," I protested.

"Out. You weren't in this theater before."

"How do you know?" I asked. "There must be three hundred people in here."

"I have ESP," he said. "Now go back to your own movie."

"This is our movie," Nate said. "We just came late. That's why you didn't see us before."

"Yeah? Where are your ticket stubs?"

All the stubs have the number of the theater on them, so you can't get into, say, Ten if your ticket says Five.

"We lost them," I said.

"When you find them you can come in."

He opened the door and practically pushed us out.

Nate glared at me as I stood there, helpless, wondering if Darlene had managed to sneak in and sit next to Warren, wondering if at this very minute she was squealing and clutching at him and hiding her gorgeous face in his satin team jacket.

"You want to try for *Young Cutthroats?*" I said glumly.

"How are we going to get into the 'R' movie if they won't even let us into the 'PG' movie?" Nate demanded.

"I don't know. I don't care. Let's just cut out."

"Oh, no. We paid good money for a movie, and I want to see a movie."

"You didn't pay," I said. *"I* paid. And you know why. Come on, Nate. I feel bad enough without sitting through another hour of toe dancing."

"We came to see a movie and I'm going to see a movie," Nate insisted. He had a sort of crazy gleam in his eye again, and I couldn't figure out why he was being so stubborn, especially since I'd had to strong-arm him into *Toujours Jeté* in the first place.

I guessed he was just paying me back. And I didn't want to get my other biceps punched. So we trudged back to Theater Five and as we stumbled down the aisle in the dark, Nate suddenly pushed me sideways into a seat behind a girl with a big frizzy mop of hair.

"Oof," I grunted and the girl turned around and said, delightedly, "Oh, hi, Hobie! I thought you didn't see me before."

And Nate cackled softly to himself while G. G. Graffman wiggled past my knees and plopped into the seat next to me.

"Now," Nate whispered, "we're even."

⤜⟨ 3 ⟩⤛

"I DIDN'T KNOW YOU LIKED BALLET, HOBIE," G. G. whispered. She had her head right next to mine, so I could hear her.

"I hate ballet." I leaned sideways, shifting in my seat before her cheek could touch my face.

"Oh," she said. Then, "Ohhh," as if she suddenly understood something.

I stared straight ahead for a few minutes, watching the screen. A woman twirled on her toes as a long red scarf unwound from her waist. A guy in tights and a satin jacket held onto one end, gathering up the scarf. Then she began twirling the other way, winding the scarf around herself again. The whole thing seemed pretty pointless.

"Would you like a Bon Bon?" G. G. held out the box.

"Thanks." I took a Bon Bon and wondered if I had just made a fatal error. Bon Bons are pretty expensive. If I ate one, did it mean I owed her anything?

I tried to watch the movie. But every once in a while I could see G. G. from the corner of my eye, sneaking glances at me. I kept shifting around in my seat, getting more and more uncomfortable. I probably looked like I had to go to the bathroom.

Finally the movie ended. I nearly leaped out of my seat and tried to push past Nate to get to the aisle. Nate had his legs stretched across the seat in front of him and didn't seem in any big hurry to leave.

"Move it, Nate."

"What's your rush?" He grinned. Lazily he lifted one foot off the back of the seat. I could feel G. G.'s hot breath on the back of my neck.

She tapped me on the shoulder. "Hobie? You want a ride home? My mother's picking me up."

"No. Nate's mother is coming for us."

"Oh." She sounded disappointed.

Nate lifted his other foot off the seat and stood up. "You can come with us," he said, looking right past me to G. G. "My mother won't mind."

"Oh, thanks!" G. G. crowed.

I gave him a look that would have made King Kong's fur stand on end. He smiled calmly and led the way out of the movies to the telephone booths in the middle of the mall.

G. G. sat next to me in the back seat of Mrs. Kramer's Datsun. I kept all the way over to my side, near the window, and wished G. G. would have the good sense to keep all the way over to her side. But she didn't. She kept edging closer and closer to me, till my only escape route was the sun roof.

Mrs. Kramer made a sharp right. I was thrown sideways, right against the back corner of the car. G. G. was thrown sideways, right against me.

"Ooops." She clutched at my jacket, maybe trying to get her balance. She smelled of chocolate and artificially buttered popcorn. I grabbed at her hands, trying to get them unclutched from my jacket. Mrs. Kramer made a sharp left.

We swung to the left and suddenly—I don't know how it happened—our hands were clasped together and my nose was flattened against G. G.'s cheek and I couldn't straighten up because her fingers were like steel clamps around mine.

"Oh, *Hobie*," she murmured.

In sheer panic I prepared to elbow her in the gut and launch myself out the sun roof, but just then the car jerked to a stop and I realized we were in front of my house.

G. G. let go of my hands. I yanked the back door open and exploded out of the car like I was shot from a cannon.

I didn't begin to relax until I was shut in my room with the lights off.

And even then I kept wanting to shove a chair under the doorknob.

I was shooting layups in the driveway the next morning when I heard Nate's voice.

"There he goes, straight for the hoop, eluding the pressing two-on-one defense—"

I whirled around. "Get off my property."

"The sidewalk is county property," Nate said. "Act your age, Hobe."

"Me? Me act my age? Get out of here."

"Aw come on, Horrible Hobe. Just consider us even."

"We were even when you dragged me back into the ballet movie and shoved me into G. G. After that ride home, I owe you one."

"Listen, that's what I came to talk to you about. You know what you were thinking about G. G.? That book she bought? And how you might be the guy she wanted to make crazy?"

"Yeah?"

"I think you were right."

I leaned against the garage door and tried to keep my eyeballs from turning up inside my lids.

"I knew it," I said. "I *knew* it. How far has she gotten in the book?"

"I don't know. She didn't say anything about the book. But she asked me if I thought you liked her."

I narrowed my eyes and glared at him, like Mac Detroit faced Don Vitello Tonnato in *Sicilian Slay Ride.* "You told her that I hated the mere sight of her, didn't you? That the thought of going out with her was enough to make me sign up with the Foreign Legion for the next twenty years? You told her something like that, right?"

"Well . . . not exactly."

"Then what, exactly?" I prepared to heave the

basketball at his head and race off to the nearest Foreign Legion recruiting office.

"I said I didn't know."

"You didn't *know?*" I heaved the basketball at his head. "What do you mean, you didn't know? I *told* you—"

"You told me she didn't really make you sick," Nate said. "So I figured you weren't sure about how you felt."

"I told you I didn't want to go out with a Marine Biologist!"

"Well, she's not a Marine Biologist yet," Nate said sarcastically. "She could always change her mind and become the waitress of your dreams."

"You know something, Nate? At the rate you're going, it'll take me ten years to get even." I slammed my hand against the garage door and wished it was Nate's face.

"Maybe eleven," Nate said nervously. "Look who's coming."

I turned around.

Down the street, riding like the wind and heading toward my house like a killer tornado, was G. G. Graffman on her trusty bike.

"I guess I'd better get home," Nate said. "See you, Hobe."

"This is all your fault!" I yelled as G. G. sped toward us. "And you're going to walk off and leave me here alone with—"

G. G. whizzed past us, past my house and up to the corner, where she made a swooping left at the cross street.

"What was that all about?" Nate said.

"Maybe she was going somewhere and this street happened to be on the way?" I cheered up a little.

"Or maybe it was just her first lap," Nate said. "Listen, it's not my fault. You're the one who swept her off her sneakers with your dazzling charm." He eyed me critically. "I can't see it myself," he added, "but there's no accounting for—"

"Here she comes again. You stay right where you are."

G. G. was heading back down the street, her knees pumping like pistons.

"She's going to wear her little toes to a nub," Nate said. He whipped his head around as she hurtled past us again, going back the way she'd originally come. "Lap two, cycle fans, and aiming for a new record!"

"What on earth is she doing?" I said. "And why is she doing it to *me?*"

"Hey, Hobe, this is getting a little repetitive. And if she ever does put her brakes on, I don't want to be here. It'll be embarrassing for her if you have to fight off her amorous advances in front of me. That's a real personal thing between a guy and a girl."

"I don't want to be around either," I said. "I'm going inside."

"See you later," Nate said. "And I still don't know what's so repulsive about G. G."

"Then *you* go with her."

"I'm not the one she wants to drive crazy," Nate

27

said. He stuck his hands in his pockets and walked off down the street.

My hand was on the doorknob when I heard a squeal of rubber, a female shriek, a clash of metal, and then a howl of pain.

Even as I turned around I told myself I shouldn't look. I should go right in the house and draw all the blinds and shove a chair under my doorknob. Because it was certainly G. G. and she had probably broken both legs and would have to be carried into my house, where she would spend six weeks with her legs in casts and nothing to do but read *How to Make Men Crazy,* and—

Sure enough, G. G. Graffman was sprawled halfway on the lawn, halfway in our driveway, tangled up in her bike. The back wheel was still spinning and G. G. was moaning softly.

Reluctantly I walked down the lawn to the scene of the accident and bent down. "Are you okay?"

"I think my shoulder—maybe my elbow too," she whimpered. "Might be broken. Am I bleeding?"

So it wasn't her legs. So it was her elbow and shoulder. She'd still spend the next six weeks in our house in traction, I thought gloomily.

I didn't see any blood, so I said, "Do you think you can stand up?" If she could stand up, she could make it to a hospital.

She grunted. "Not till you get the bike off me."

Carefully I gripped the handlebars, grabbed the seat, and lifted the bike away from G. G. I pushed it onto the grass. "Can you get up now?"

"I think so. If you'll just pull me up *very gently*." She held out her hand.

This is all a plot, I thought, to get me to hold her hand. But anything to get her on her feet and out of my life.

I took her hand and pulled.

"Gently!" she screamed. She made it to her knees, then stood up, shakily.

"Ohh, Hobie," she groaned. She sagged against me. I panicked and grabbed her shoulders to push her away.

"Ouch! Hobie, that hurts!"

I let go of her shoulders and she sagged right back into me again. A point on the collar of her down vest poked me in the nose.

A nine-year-old neighbor who I'd always thought was a good kid zipped by on a skateboard. "Hobie's got a girlfriend, Hobie's got a girlfriend!"

G. G. was still using my chest as a leaning post and my shoulder as a pillow. It looked like we were going to be standing there forever, and I began to plan in what order I wanted to terminate people. Nate first, or G. G.?

"Do you, Hobie?" G. G. asked. She finally managed to tear herself away from me.

I quickly backed away before she could lean on me again. "Do I what?"

G. G. didn't look at me, but concentrated on the shoulder she was gently rubbing. "Have a girlfriend?"

Now what? Before the panic could set in again I asked myself what Mac Detroit would do in a situation like this. Simple. He'd either grab her and kiss her lips which were like ripe fruit or push her out of his hotel room with a terse but pithy put-down, such as, "Sorry, Sweetheart, I've got other flounders to fillet."

Neither option was viable, since the first was out of the question and the second required a hotel room to push G. G. out of. I began to wonder if Mac Detroit had ever faced a really dangerous situation like this one, or if he merely spent his days flirting with death.

"Listen, G. G., that was a pretty bad fall you had. You'd better get right home and lie down." I didn't care whether she went to bed or hung from the dining room chandelier, as long as she did it at her house. "And be careful!"

"I was being careful," she said. "I was just trying to do a wheelie."

"A *wheelie?* At your age?" I didn't want to prolong the conversation, but I really was sur-prised—even if G. G. was immature. At least I'd gotten her mind off my love life and onto her bike. Now if I could only get *G. G.* onto her bike . . .

"I know, I know. It was stupid. But it wasn't all my fault. I think you have a crack in your driveway. And I only did it to—I mean—I haven't tried a wheelie in years. I just wanted—well, you *did* no-tice me."

I hadn't gotten her mind off me at all. But I felt a little less nervous; it really was just a matter of saying, "Scram, sweetheart, I have other chickens to fricassee," and that would be that.

30

"All right," I said gruffly. "I noticed you. The whole block noticed you. Now. scram, sweetheart, I have other chickens to fricassee."

She stared at me, her eyes all round and her mouth slightly open. She knew a brush-off when she heard one, I thought, elated. Maybe old Mac Detroit really does have all the answers!

"Oh, Hobie . . . ," she sighed.

"Whaaat?" I snarled. "What now?"

"Hobie . . . you called me sweetheart!"

❦ 4 ❧

IT WAS MY THEORY THAT G. G. WAS VERY IMMA-
ture for her age. Physically and emotionally. I'm
sure my father thinks *I'm* very immature for my
age, but he has limited contact with teenagers,
whereas I mingle with them every day of my life.

Having made an in-depth study of female teenagers at close range—as close as I could get, anyway—I can tell you that G. G.'s emotional development and social skills were definitely deficient. We
won't even discuss her hair.

While other fourteen-year-old girls were doing
normal things like shopping for clothes and snickering about boys behind our backs and trying on
lipsticks (I work at the Million Dollar Mall, so I
know what I'm talking about), G. G. was hanging
around the marina asking boat owners if they had
any spare barnacles she could study.

Naturally I don't expect girls to focus entirely on
their looks and the pursuit of boyfriends, but I don't

expect them to focus entirely on obscure fish facts either.

I mean, boys care about how they look too. I want my jeans to fit right and my hair to be clean in case anybody wants to run their fingers through it, and a zit smack on the bridge of my nose is no laughing matter.

This is normal. Remember, I work in a bookstore. I am surrounded by psychology books. I *know*.

Part of G. G.'s problem may have been that she wasn't just immature for her age, but young for her grade. She started school early because her parents realized she had a world-class brain, so she wasn't even fourteen yet. Maybe a couple of months really make a difference at that age.

But last year, when Darlene was thirteen, she was already reading *Cosmo* and putting on lipstick in the lunchroom with a little mirror held up to her mouth.

There was no doubt in my mind that G. G. was one of your late bloomers, but now, all of a sudden, she looked like she was trying real hard to bloom. Right in my own front yard.

Why me? I had no idea. All I knew was that if G. G. pursued me with the same single-minded determination she had—up till now—pursued jellyfish, my ass was eelgrass.

Darlene was in my English class and when I walked past her desk Monday morning she was brushing her hair and tossing it around, so that Nate kept ducking to keep from getting hit in the face by flying hair. For the hundred and thirty-third time I wished I had the desk in back of Darlene.

"Hey, Darlene," I said nonchalantly, "that was some disappearing act you pulled at the movies. What happened to you girls?" It wasn't killer wit, but at least my voice didn't crack.

Nate bent his head back and stared up at the ceiling to show me he wasn't eavesdropping.

"We just decided to see a different movie," Darlene said. She was no slouch at nonchalance either. She smiled, sort of privately, as if there was some secret meaning behind her words.

It was no big secret to me. I guessed she had managed to find Warren Adler in Theater Six. I didn't want to guess what had happened after that.

She swept her hair back from her cheek. Her fingernails were silver. Her sweater was pink and soft and fuzzy. Her posture was excellent.

I decided I'd better get to my seat.

I work in Bookathon Monday, Wednesday, and Friday afternoons and all day Saturday. Monday is generally a pretty slow day, especially during my hours, so I have time to read or do homework.

That afternoon it was raining and business was not booming. In between a few sales I had time to finish *Terminate with Extreme Pain* and do some creative imagining about how Mac Detroit would get Darlene to like him. Actually, you didn't have to be too creative to figure it out. He'd grab her and kiss her lips which were like ripe fruit and that would be that. Mac Detroit never had to get women to like him. That came with the territory.

At five to five G. G. tromped in.

Damp red curls stuck to her forehead and I could hear her sneakers squishing as she walked.

"Hi, Hobie." Did I imagine her eyelashes fluttering? "I left my bike outside. I got a new lock."

"Good," I said. "But would you please get back from the magazines? You're dripping all over them."

She biked here? In the pouring rain? With no raincoat, no hat, nothing?

"But I want to pick one out," she said. "What am I supposed to do, stand on the other side of the store and use binoculars?"

A little touch of hostility there. Fine with me. But I couldn't help thinking she had gone to an awful lot of trouble through an awful lot of water just to buy a magazine.

"Well, you could stand back a little bit, couldn't you? And when you pick one out I'll get it for you."

She thought about it for a minute. "I guess so," she said slowly. I don't know what there was to think about, but like I said, G. G. was none too swift about some things.

She stepped back from the magazine racks and then leaned forward, her chin jutting out as she peered at the titles. A woman who'd been browsing in the back came up to the counter with a $3.50 paperback and got extremely huffy when I told her she couldn't use her Visa card on purchases under ten dollars.

35

She slammed the book down on the counter and stalked out.

"My, you get all kinds," G. G. said. "You must know a lot about people, working here."

"Yeah."

"And life," she went on. "You must have a lot of experience."

I couldn't deny that, especially since she didn't specify what kind of experience, and while I didn't want to encourage her by responding to her conversational ploys, it certainly wouldn't hurt to agree that I knew my way around. The information might—somehow—get back to Darlene.

"You better believe it, sw—" I nearly called her "sweetheart," but stopped myself just in time. "You better believe it."

"Well, I know what I want. Would you get me— uh—*Cosmo, Glamour,* and *Road and Track.*"

Oh, brother. First, *How to Make Men Crazy,* now *Cosmo* and *Glamour.* This girl was aiming to bloom so fast I was going to end up smothered in petals.

The *Road and Track* didn't fool me a bit. People do that all the time. They buy a book with a really steamy cover and then a copy of, say, *The Brothers Karamazov,* so you won't think they're total degenerates.

I rang up the magazines and stuck them in a bag. They'd probably be soaked by the time G. G. got them home. I hoped so. One of the titles on the *Cosmo* was "Lure Him to Your Web—Seduction Secrets of Black Widow Spiders."

I tried to turn off my creative imagination on that one. Some things are just too horrible to contemplate.

"Well, see you later, Hobie," G. G. said.

She didn't look dangerous. Actually she just looked sort of wet and droopy. But she didn't walk briskly out the door, either, and I began to get nervous again. It must have been those spider seduction secrets—I had an urge to dive under the counter.

"See you. Gotta get to work," I said. I walked toward the stockroom in back. It was just as good a place to hide as under the counter, and a lot more dignified. I was almost there when I heard G. G.'s sneakers squishing out the door.

I was standing right in front of the Psychology and Self-Help books. *How to Make Men Crazy* was prominently displayed in the center of the rack. I pulled out a copy and looked at the table of contents. Know your enemy, I thought, and maybe you can keep one step ahead of her.

Providing she's not a speed reader.

I went back to the counter and started skimming until I got to a section called "Accidental Meetings."

"Back in the old days, a woman used to drop her handkerchief in front of a man she wanted to meet. The gentleman would reach down and pick it up, thus an apparently chance incident would bring them together. Modern women don't use handkerchiefs much anymore—and few men would stoop

down to pick up a used Kleenex—but there are
ways to adapt this principle to contemporary court-
ship."

The writing wasn't very zippy, but the subject
matter was riveting. I sensed I was about to learn
something vital to my health and well-being.

"Many minor mishaps have (literally) thrown
people together—you might trip or stumble right in
front of an attractive stranger. You might get your
dog's leash tangled up with his dog's leash, or
'accidentally' tip over his drink at the bar. . . ."

I groaned and closed the book. I finally knew
what Mac Detroit meant when he said, "My gut felt
like a block of ice."

I could see it plainly, and it made my gut feel like
a block of ice. "You might trip or stumble. . . ." Or
fall off your bike. G. G.'s accident yesterday had
been no accident. She did it on purpose, not just so
I'd notice her, but so I'd have to talk to her and hold
her hand and help her up.

Suddenly I could foresee a whole series of staged
"accidents." G. G. would trip in the lunchroom and
drop a tray full of food in my lap. And herself after
it. G. G. would come into Bookathon and "accidentally" knock over an intricately pyramided stack of
The Des Moines Diet and I'd have to go over and
pick them all up and she'd fall down in the middle of
the pile and I'd have to pick *her* up too.

The opportunities for disaster were limitless,
given G. G.'s chart-busting I.Q. and her apparent
determination to lure me into her web.

And as I pictured the gruesome scenarios, I could

see Darlene in every picture, standing off to one side, witnessing my humiliation, her lips like ripe fruit parted in a sweet, mocking smile.

Alone in my room that night I tried to write a poem to Darlene. I did that sometimes. Nobody knew about it. Especially not Darlene. I never sent them. I never wanted to write a poem until I noticed Darlene. I didn't even like poetry.

> *Your skin like silk,*
> *Your hair like new-mown wheat,*
> *Your teeth as white as milk . . .*

I got stuck there. All I could think of for the next line was "Your delicate little feet," and that was sickening. Besides which, I never noticed her feet. Her legs, yes, but not her feet.

My parents were downstairs. I went into their room and dialed Darlene's number. She had her own phone. I knew, because it was listed in the phone book.

"Hello?" Darlene's voice purred in my ear.

I felt my ear vibrate.

I hung up.

I did that sometimes too.

I suddenly wondered if my emotional development and social skills were any more evolved than G. G.'s.

I went back to my room and looked at the poem. I had no idea what the color of new-mown wheat was, but half the women in the Mac Detroit books have hair like it. I was pretty sure it was blonde, but Darlene probably wouldn't know what new-mown wheat looked like either, even if she ever did read my poem.

Which she wouldn't, because I'd never send it.

What I ought to do, I told myself, is *send* it. Or give it to her in person. Not this one, which wasn't turning out very well, but a really good one. What I really should do, I knew, was ask her if she wanted to go to the movies or something, but I didn't think I was ready for that yet.

Even though I'm not your basic introverted type, it was hard enough for me to get off one nonchalant sentence to her. But ask her out? Just like that? I couldn't do it. Why in the world would Darlene DeVries want to go out with me?

What if she laughed? Just stood there, laughing at me, like the idea was too ridiculous for words. I couldn't stand it. I couldn't face the possibility of that laughter. As long as I didn't ask, she couldn't say no. She couldn't make me feel like I wanted to crawl under a rock. As long as I didn't try, I could imagine that she might go out with me someday, that she might even secretly like me.

Oh, sure, I was afraid of being rejected, I knew that much. I mean, I didn't read all those psychology books for nothing. But understanding why I was afraid didn't make me any less afraid.

Plus which, now that Darlene probably had a crush on Warren Adler, it seemed more unrealistic than ever that she'd be interested in me.

Warren Adler is six feet two inches tall. And

muscular, with shoulders like a football player—
except that he plays basketball, so you can see he's
not wearing shoulder pads.

I trudged downstairs. My father was in the den,
reading and watching TV at the same time.

"I thought I might start working out again," I said
casually.

"That's a good idea," he said. "Do you want me
to help you put the weights together?"

"Great. You want to do it now?"

"Why not?" He sounded almost cheerful.

My mother looked up from the TV and beamed at
him.

He put his book down on the couch. I caught a
glimpse of the title before he stood up, clapped a
hand on my shoulder and headed for the basement
door.

The book was *How to Talk to Your Teenager.*

5

THE NEXT FEW DAYS WERE UNEVENTFUL. G. G. didn't drop a tray on me in the lunchroom or wreak havoc at Bookathon or accidentally fall off our roof.

In spite of this—or maybe because of it—I began to get really tense. Like Mac Detroit, I imagined danger was lurking around every corner, disaster always moments away. I kept looking back over my shoulder, constantly fearing that G. G. would suddenly leap out from nowhere and drag me to her web, where she would subject my helpless person to all the hideous secrets she had learned from black widow spiders.

"She's too quiet," I told Nate. "She's laying back, planning something *really big*."

"Maybe she's just studying," Nate said. "She hasn't made you crazy yet, so she's boning up on the basics."

"What do you mean, she hasn't made me crazy

yet? She's turned me paranoid. Isn't that crazy enough for you?"

Nate patted my shoulder consolingly. "For me, yes. For her, no."

I worked out with my father every evening, and he didn't say a word about college or careers. I told myself that as soon as I built myself up a little, and wrote the perfect poem for Darlene, I'd have enough confidence to let her know how I felt. I told myself that all she could do was reject me, so I had a fifty-fifty chance of success.

Plus, lots of girls think poetry is romantic, and Darlene might be so overcome by my romanticness that she'd begin to think that Warren Adler was a muscle-bound clod compared to me.

Friday, when I got to Bookathon, my grandfather asked me if I could work an extra hour, because Jennifer, who usually starts work at six, had a dentist appointment and would be late.

"Sure. I'll stay till closing if you want." I do that sometimes on Fridays, because it's usually pretty busy.

"If you've got nothing else to do," Grandpa said, "that would be a help."

"I don't have anything else to do," I said glumly. Except write poems to Darlene, who would probably be in the Million Dollar Multiplex trying to snuggle up to Warren Adler's oversized shoulder.

Grandpa gave me an inquisitive look but didn't push it.

We were pretty busy for most of the afternoon, so when Jennifer showed up a half hour earlier than she'd expected, Grandpa took the opportunity to go get something to eat.

There was a line of about eight people at the registers and Jennifer and I were both ringing up orders as fast as we could when Darlene strolled into the store. She was carrying bags from Bizarre Boutique and Stage Door Cosmetics and she was wearing a gray suede jacket and tight jeans and boots, and I nearly rolled the credit card imprinter over my thumb when I saw her.

Darlene doesn't come into Bookathon very often—I don't think she's one of your heavy readers—and she was *alone* this time. No Shawna or Lesley to stand around looking bored or scornful at my conversational ploys.

"Be back in a minute," I muttered to Jennifer. I ignored her glare and the irritable expressions of the people on line. I nearly vaulted over the counter, but I thought better of it at the last minute. I didn't want to plow feet-first into the customers, as Darlene would probably think that was not cool.

"Hey there, Darlene." I caught up with her at the Romance rack. "Can I help you with something?"

"Hi, Hobie." She had a lot of lipstick on and her lips were shiny and moist-looking. I got this sudden, intense craving for a piece of ripe fruit.

Two other women were browsing through the romances but I didn't pay any attention to them and hoped they would show me the same courtesy.

"What are you looking for?" I asked Darlene.

"*Wild, Wanton Love,*" she said.

Oh, so am I, I thought crazily.

"Here it is." I reached up to take it out of the rack. I tried not to sweat. I handed Darlene the book, hoping that our fingers would touch, but they didn't. Darlene flipped through it, stopped at page forty-four and started to read, moving her moist fuchsia lips as she concentrated.

Distantly I heard the bell at the front counter going "ping, ping" which meant I was needed, but I had more urgent needs of my own. I hovered over Darlene till she closed the book.

"Can I ring that up for you?" I asked. I tried to sound cool and professional. Helpful but not pushy. I inched closer to her. She turned around to study the racks again and her hair swirled against my face.

I told myself that men don't faint, only women faint, then felt my knees buckle and waited for everything to go black. It didn't. I could still hear the bell up front, and if Jennifer didn't stop whacking that thing I was going to do something drastic.

"No, it's too long," Darlene was saying. "I want something with less pages."

"Less pages. Right. Let's see. . . . The 'Eternal Embers' line is very popular. Ever read any of those? They're real short; none of that historical junk."

"Have you got *Flaming Desire?*" Darlene asked.

One more question like that and I'd be gnawing on the software.

"You bet. Right over here. That's a different line. Very contemporary. For today's woman."

Suddenly Jennifer was tapping sharply on my shoulder. "Hobie, there are fourteen peop—"

Darlene turned around to glance at Jennifer and then seemed to lose interest. She moved further down the aisle.

"Oh," Jennifer said. I don't know if it was Darlene's violet eyes or my expression of extreme anguish that tipped her off, but she just whispered, "Hurry up, okay? It's a zoo up there."

I shot her a grateful look and trotted after Darlene. *"Flaming Desire* Number Fourteen is supposed to be good. We sell a lot of those." Helpful but not pushy, I reminded myself. Cool. Professional. Mac Detroit.

Mac Detroit had probably never been in a bookstore in his life, but we were talking style here, not substance.

Darlene turned around and looked at me vaguely, almost like she was going to say, "Oh. Are you still here?"

Which is practically what she said. "Look, I'm just sort of browsing. You don't have to help me. I might not even buy anything. I just told Shawna to meet me here when she was finished shopping."

My shoulders sagged. I tried to think of something else to say so I could keep talking to her, but she was already rounding a corner to the next row.

I walked slowly back to the counter and moved in next to Jennifer. I didn't say anything, just took the books from the next person in line and began to ring up the sale.

A couple of the customers made some loud remarks about how poor service was these days and how long they'd been standing in line. What they were really doing was yelling at me without actually yelling at me. This way they wouldn't feel rude or guilty about picking on a poor, underpaid teenager.

I didn't care. I handed a customer his bag and noticed that Shawna had come into the store and was looking around for Darlene.

I took the next person in line, who was charging his books, and while he signed the slip and put his address on it, I saw Darlene and Shawna heading for the door.

They were talking loudly and giggling, and as I handed the man his bag of books I thought maybe Darlene was telling Shawna about how I trailed around after her in the store, but it turned out they were only talking about something Shawna had bought at the Sweet Dreams shop.

Things slowed down after that and by five forty-five Bookathon was practically empty. Jennifer reached under the counter for her pocketbook and took out some tissues and a lipstick. There was a little mirror on the flap of her purse.

"So, how's it going?" she asked. She peered into the mirror and applied fresh lipstick.

"Could be worse."

Jennifer snapped her purse shut. "You really like her, don't you?"

I shrugged.

Jennifer and I talk from time to time, but we don't often work the same hours, and up till now our talk had been fairly general. I did know some personal things about her, like how her boyfriend wanted to be an actor and her mother thought he was an unrealistic dreamer who would never earn a living. And I'd told her how my father felt pretty much the same way about me. She was sympathetic and said I had lots of time to think about things like that before I had to make a career decision.

I avoided her question about Darlene. "My father's sort of loosening up. That's something. He's reading this book called *How to Talk to Your Teenager*. I think he's really trying."

"That's great," Jennifer said.

"I wonder why they don't write books for teenagers called *How to Talk to Your Parents.*"

Jennifer laughed. "Maybe because teenagers don't want to talk to their parents. They'd rather talk to other teenagers. . . . She's really got you spinning your wheels, hasn't she?"

Suddenly I found myself telling Jennifer the whole, sordid, depressing story. Not just about my hopeless crush on Darlene, and her crush on Warren, but about G. G. and her hopeless crush on me, and the terrific contrast between the girl of my dreams and the marine biologist of my nightmares.

I didn't tell her about the poems, though.

Jennifer shook her head and smiled. "Look at it this way. You must have it—whatever 'it' is—or G. G. wouldn't be so—um—ardent."

"If I've got it, how come Darlene doesn't see it?"

"But that's a crummy book G. G. is reading," Jennifer mused. "You know what she really ought to read?"

I didn't care. All I wanted to know was, how do I let Darlene see that I have "it?" Whatever "it" is.

"She really ought to read *Love's Gender Trap: Attitudinal Differences between Men and Women*. It really helped me understand Brent."

"I don't *want* G. G. to understand me," I said. "Look, Jennifer, you're a good-looking girl—"

"Woman," Jennifer corrected me.

"Woman. You must have known lots of guys."

She looked sort of amused. "Tons," she agreed.

"Well, the ones you really liked. What did you like about them? How did they act?"

Jennifer looked thoughtful for a moment. "You know, that's a good question. I never analyzed it."

"Analyze it now," I urged. "What kind of a guy do you think Darlene would like?"

"I don't know what Darlene would like. You can't generalize about these things, Hobie. All women are different."

"I know, I know."

"But maybe—maybe guys who are secure; comfortable with themselves. Who know what they want. Self-confident, you know? So they don't have to put me down to build themselves up. I like someone who knows what he wants and goes out and gets it. I don't like wishy-washy."

"You sound like my father," I said.

"Sorry about that."

"And G. G.? What about her? How can I get her off my case?"

Jennifer shrugged. "She can't get you if you don't want to be gotten, can she? I mean, she can try, but the ultimate decision is yours. You're in control here, whether you realize it or not."

I thought about that for a minute. "I guess you're right." I was sort of surprised to realize it. "She can't *make* me love her."

"No, she can't. But listen, Hobie. Don't be a creep about it. Be a man."

"What do you mean?"

"You don't want Darlene to hurt you. Don't you hurt G. G. either. She's taking real scary risks, letting you know how she feels. Don't shoot her down too hard."

I sighed. "I don't know if anything else will work with G. G. She doesn't discourage as easy as some people."

"Hobie, don't turn into someone I won't like. You can discourage a person without destroying her."

"How?" I sounded desperate. "She could end up destroying *me*."

"No," Jennifer said firmly. "But Darlene could. If you let her."

❧ 6 ❧

I WORKED IN THE STORE ON SATURDAY AND SPENT Saturday night and Sunday doing my homework and writing poems to Darlene.

I went out for a while on Sunday, just to ride around a bit on my bike. I happened to pass Darlene's house a couple of times and slowed down, but she wasn't outside. Considering it was thirty degrees and I had to fight a raw, damp wind as I pedaled, I wasn't too surprised that she was not romping around on her front lawn.

I pictured her in her room, curled up on her bed, reading one of my poems. I pictured her lips like ripe fruit forming each word of love she had inspired, then sighing and pressing the poem against her heart.

Then I told myself I was a moron and rode home—against the wind all the way.

Monday morning G. G. Graffman was waiting for me at the door to my homeroom. She had done something to her hair. She was wearing a shiny bright green shirt that made her eyes look even greener, like emeralds or something.

"Hi, Hobie," she said breathlessly. She sounded like one of the girls on the *Cosmo* covers.

This is it! Phase two of Operation Make Me Crazy was underway.

"Notice anything different about me?" She leaned against the wall and gazed into my eyes, like she was trying to hypnotize me. Like, say, a spider hypnotizes a tasty-looking fly.

"Uh, no. Gotta go in now."

"The bell won't ring for another five minutes," she said. "What's your hurry?" She used that husky voice again.

Someone jostled me as he went into the room, pushing me toward G. G. Was that perfume I smelled?

I swallowed a few times and clutched my books against my hip. She did look different. Not great, you understand, but different. The perfume didn't stink either. But she was still no Darlene DeVries. And I still didn't want to be the object of her juvenile crush. I didn't want her blooming all over *me*.

I backed away. "I have some stuff to do."

G. G. lowered her eyes. Her shoulders slumped a little.

I remembered what Jennifer had said on Friday about not being a creep. Maybe I couldn't help it that G. G. found me—for some reason—irresistible, but that didn't mean I had to be cruel.

"Uh—your hair looks nice," I said.

"Do you think so?" she said eagerly. "I got it cut on Saturday, but I was really nervous because I never—"

Holy cow. She moved closer to me, chattering about her hair. Who cared about her hair? I'd just been trying to let her down easy, and here I'd gotten her all wound up again.

"See you, G. G. Gotta go."

I ducked into the room and practically ran to my desk. I yanked open my Earth Science book and buried my head in it until the bell rang.

G. G. was waiting for me outside my homeroom again when the last bell rang. I pretended not to see her. But she saw me.

"Hobie! Hobie!"

I sprinted down the hall with my jacket slung over my shoulder and my books banging against my hip. I bounced off a couple of people, sidestepped an open locker door, and generally acted as uncool as possible.

All I could think of was escape. I thought I could hear G. G.'s Nikes pounding behind me, but that was crazy. The halls were full of kids heading for freedom; a herd of thundering elephants couldn't have made a dent in that din.

I zoomed down the front steps of the school and when I hit the bottom step she was right beside me, matching me stride for stride. Either working out was doing me very little good, or she'd gone into training herself.

"You better put your jacket on, Hobie. You'll catch cold."

A cold sounded like a good idea. Pneumonia would be even better. Anything that would keep me safely in my room until G. G. finished blooming or found someone else to make crazy.

"Why were you running?" she asked. "Didn't you see me?"

Sure, sweetheart, why do you think I was running? That's what Mac Detroit would have said. But I couldn't say it without being the type of person Jennifer wouldn't like, and Jennifer was my only source of information about women. Except for Mac Detroit. I didn't think Jennifer would like Mac Detroit at all.

Then I remembered that I'd tried not to be mean to G. G. this morning and it had gotten me in deeper. Maybe Jennifer wasn't completely objective when it came to male-female relationships. I mean, she had her own webs to spin.

"Are you working today?" G. G. trudged along beside me.

"Yeah, that's why I was running. So I wouldn't be late." *Don't explain!* That just encourages her. Mac Detroit never explains anything.

"I'll walk to the mall with you," G. G. said. "I have some shopping to do."

Shopping? First the book, then *Cosmo*, then the haircut and now shopping? Had my mysterious charm made G. G. so crazy that she had completely given up mollusks for me?

"It's a long walk," I said gruffly.

"No it's not."

"It's too cold to walk."

"Oh, Hobie! I never realized how you worried about me. That's so sweet."

I felt like I was digging my grave with my tongue.

"Hobie?"

"What?"

"What do you want to do with your life?"

"What?"

"I mean, when you get older. What do you want to be?"

"You too?" I said. "You sound just like my father. How come everyone is so interested in my future all of a sudden?"

"Don't bite my head off," G. G. said. "I just wanted to know what you're interested in, that's all."

I'll bet. I'll just bet. The old "get a man talking about himself" ploy.

Right now I was interested in getting rid of G. G. and getting hold of Darlene DeVries; for a minute I thought I might tell her that, but I didn't. Nobody knew about Darlene and me except Nate, and even he didn't know how bad I had it.

"Look, kid, I don't feel much like talking right now, okay?" I made my voice rough, like Humphrey Bogart. I thought calling her "kid" would give her a clue as to how I felt about her.

"I understand," she said. "Sometimes two people can be together and not have to say a word."

I groaned in despair.

"Are you all right, Hobie?" G. G. sounded extremely concerned.

"No!" I said. *"No!"*

WHY ME?

Your eyes the bluest of all blue
Your skin the fairest of the fair,
Oh, let me spend one hour with you,
Entwining rosebuds in your hair.

Not bad. A little gloppy, definitely too faggy, but I was getting there.

Unless rosebuds had thorns, in which case Darlene would end up with scalp wounds.

My heart cries out to yours. . . .

No good. Nothing rhymes with "yours."

Your heart cries out to mine. . . .

No it doesn't. If it did, I wouldn't be sitting here writing these stupid poems.

Kiss me once and let me dream
About the sweetness of your kiss
And if we never meet again
Then once I will have tasted bliss.

I stared in disbelief at the paper.

Did *I* write that?

"Hobie?"

"Yeah, Dad?"

"You want to work out now? I need some exercise."

By George, I thought I had it—the perfect poem.

WHY ME?

I stuffed the whole batch of poems I'd been working on into my notebook and dropped it on my desk.

Now all I had to do was build up my biceps.

I charged out of the room and clapped my father heartily on the shoulder, almost like I was the father and he was the son. "You got it," I said. "And I'll bet I press forty pounds tonight."

❧ 7 ❧

TUESDAY AFTERNOON WHEN I WALKED PAST Darlene's desk she was drawing hearts on the cover of her English book. Little hearts, joined together, with an arrow through them. There were initials in the centers of the hearts. None of the initials were mine.

I hadn't pressed forty pounds last night either.

I leaned over Nate's desk. "Have you seen G. G.? Did you see what she did to herself?"

"Yeah. She looks nice."

"You know why, don't you? She walked me to the mall yesterday. She waited by my homeroom in the morning. She's closing in for the kill."

"Hey, hey, calm yourself, big fella. It's only round one, you know."

"Nate, that girl isn't fooling around. Did you see her yet today? She wasn't waiting for me this morning, and I'm worried."

"Gee, you miss her already?"

"Stuff it, Nate. I'm just trying to keep one step ahead of her, that's all."

"I did see her for a minute at lunch. She ate a hearty meal."

"Probably wants to keep her strength up," I muttered.

"By the way, Hobe—" Nate reached into his pocket and took out a tiny folded piece of paper. "She asked me to give you this."

He dropped the note into my hand and smiled innocently.

Hobie—I must see you. It's urgent. I have something very important to tell you. I'll meet you outside your room after the last bell. It's a matter of Life and Death.

GGG

My gut felt like a block of ice.

Nate was laughing so hard he had to hold his sides.

How could I be best friends with someone who had such a perverted sense of humor?

By two-thirty, when the last bell rang, I was already zipping down Van Buren Street and halfway home. I'd never even stuck my head through the door of my homeroom. Mr. Schulman might discover that I'd cut out early, but what else could I do?

WHY ME?

As Mac Detroit says, if you walk into an ambush with your eyes wide open, you deserve to be carried out with your eyes shut tight.

My whole life was starting to feel like an ambush waiting to happen. G. G. wasn't going to give me a moment's peace until I let her make me crazy, and I'd have to be out of my mind if I let her make me crazy.

Go figure that one out, sports fans.

Wednesday afternoon I was sitting in Earth Science experiencing extreme nervous tension. And not because of the surprise quiz we were taking.

I hadn't seen G. G. all day, and after ignoring her urgent message yesterday, I wondered why she hadn't made some effort to catch up with me.

Why wasn't she lingering outside my house that morning, waiting to pounce on me the minute I walked out the door? Why hadn't she been leaning seductively against my homeroom door when I got to school, or stalking me down the halls? Why hadn't she called me last night to ask why I hadn't met her when it was a matter of life and death?

The suspense was killing me. I had this really big thing built up in my mind about how she'd corner me someplace where there was no escape, probably in front of a large number of people, including Darlene, and do something that would humiliate me. I couldn't imagine what it might be—but I was sure it was going to happen.

Ms. Goulding was just reading the fourth question of the surprise quiz—and it was a surprise to me that I knew the first three answers—when the door opened and G. G. walked in.

It was starting. I *knew* it. Duck under the desk? Jump out a window? Impossible. I was trapped. I hunched over my quiz paper, knowing perfectly well that this would not make me invisible.

G. G. handed Ms. Goulding a note. Ms. Goulding frowned. "We're right in the middle of a quiz," she said to G. G. "Can't this wait?"

G. G. shook her head. "She said right away. She said it was important."

"All right. Hobie Katz, Mrs. Elliott wants to see you. In the library. You'd better take your books."

Mrs. Elliott? The librarian? I hardly ever go into the library. Why would Mrs. Elliott want to see me? She wouldn't even know my name.

I picked up my books and dropped my unfinished quiz paper on Ms. Goulding's desk.

"Come in this afternoon and make up the rest," she said.

"I have to work this afternoon."

"All right, see me tomorrow." Ms. Goulding turned back to her questions.

I followed G. G. out the door.

"What's going on?" I demanded. "What does Mrs. Elliott want to see me about?"

"Something about an overdue book, I think. I'm not sure."

"Wait a minute, wait a minute. I never took out any books from this library. How can there be an overdue book?"

"I don't know," G. G. said. "Maybe somebody

used your name. Come on." She grabbed hold of my arm and pulled.

I shook her hand off. She was wearing perfume again. Her cheeks were very rosy. "You don't have to take me," I said. "I know the way."

"I have to go back anyway," G. G. said. "I work in the library this period. I'm a student aide."

Something strange was going on here. I sensed an ambush in the making, I felt that this was the Biggie that G. G. had planned. But there was the note Mrs. Elliott had written. I couldn't explain *that*.

I started walking down the hall real fast, taking big strides, trying to keep far ahead of G. G. But as usual, she was too fast for me. I thought about how I'd tried to keep one step ahead of her in her plan to make me crazy, and I laughed inwardly—a bitter, cynical laugh.

G. G. was right on my heels when I opened the door to the library. There were some kids at the tables, hunched over books and papers, but I didn't see Mrs. Elliott. I wasn't even sure I'd recognize her, but I didn't see anyone who looked like a librarian, so I headed for the office in the back.

"Hobie," G. G. whispered. "Wait a minute. Before you talk to Mrs. Elliott there's something I'd better tell you."

I knew it, I knew it. Don't panic, Katz, just keep walking. Only, ditch the tail. Get away from G. G. I veered left, toward the encyclopedias, and stopped short.

Darlene DeVries was sitting at a table in the

reference section. Her head was bent over a book, her hair like new-mown wheat just brushing the pages.

Lucky book, I thought wildly, and then remembered I had to shake G. G.

"Hobie, *please*," G. G. hissed. "You're going to get in trouble. So am I, if you don't just listen a minute."

She dragged me into a corner of the reference section. I let her. Suddenly I felt numb, like I couldn't fight anymore. I could see the back of Darlene's head and smell G. G.'s perfume and feel all the energy go out of me. They'd carry me out with my eyes shut tight and drop me in the middle of G. G.'s web.

I felt dizzy. Weak. Confused. *Trapped.*

My eyes began to water and itch. I'm getting sick, I thought, that's why I feel so weak. She got me when my resistance was low, my defenses down.

I sneezed. Probably getting the flu.

"Gesundheit," G. G. whispered. "Hobie, listen. Mrs. Elliott didn't send for you."

"What?" I sneezed again. Darlene looked up from her book.

"Gesundheit," G. G. said. "I was desperate. When you didn't meet me yesterday I didn't know what else to do."

"What are you talking about?" A whole volley of sneezes now. Darlene looked up again, twisted her head around and saw me. She wiggled two delicate, tapered fingers at me. I waved my handkerchief back at her and tried not to sneeze. My face felt hot. I'm not sure if it was because of Darlene or invading germs.

"But the note," I said. Was the room tilting, or what? "She wrote that note. Ahhh—CHOO!"

"Gesundheit. No she didn't. I forged it."

❦ 8 ❧

THE ROOM *WAS* TILTING. OR I WAS DELIRIOUS AND hadn't heard right. G. G. Graffman, model student, devoted follower of kelp and carp, (formerly) innocent child, forging a teacher's signature? Shanghaiing me out of class in total defiance of school rules and plain old self-preservation?

Had I, Hobie Katz, driven her to this?

Or was *Cosmo* responsible?

In *Slay Ride in Sicily,* Don Vitello Tonnato has Mac Detroit drugged, slipping him some mind-altering substance that turns his mind to mush and his perceptions to Silly Putty.

I knew just how he felt.

I groped for the nearest chair and fell into it.

I sneezed.

"Gesundheit." G. G. pulled a chair right next to me and bent her head so our noses were almost touching. She was so crazed by passion that she was not only risking expulsion from school and the shattering of her whole future as a marine biologist, but serious infection to boot.

"Hobie, let's be honest with each other," G. G. said. "I mean, the essence of a good relationship is honest communication."

I choked. My eyes felt like they were on fire. I slid my chair back away from her. She slid her chair toward me. She was closing in for the kill. I was already dying.

"What relationship?" I gasped. "What are you doing to me? Why did you forge that note?"

"It's the only way I could be sure you'd talk to me. Maybe it's my imagination, but you seem to be avoiding me."

"It's not your imagination!" I started chain sneezing. I thought I was going to blow a hole through my handkerchief.

"Gesundheit. Look, Hobie, maybe you don't love me right this moment—"

"Love you? *Love You?*" I slid my chair back so far I hit the shelf of *Britannicas* in the corner. I looked around frantically. Darlene was watching us. She was smiling with amusement, her lips, like ripe fruit—

G. G. pulled her chair right up to mine again. Trapped, completely trapped. I'd backed myself into a corner.

Darlene wasn't the only one watching us. There were lots of curious stares in our direction. It was all happening, exactly the nightmare I'd imagined.

". . . but I'm a very determined person," G. G. was saying. "I get what I want. And I want *you*."

Oh my God.

"I don't know why I love you, Hobie. You're not superbright. You don't have any outstanding talents. You're certainly not what I'd call a hunk—"

"Wait a minute, wait a minute! Aachoo!" This was too much. Here she's telling me she loves me, and she reels off a list of all the reasons why I'm not lovable? What kind of crazy advice was she reading in *How to Make Men Crazy?*

"Gesundheit. Maybe it's chemistry or something. I don't know. It's a mystery to me. And you're a mystery too. I mean, when you sat next to me in the movies, even though you said you hated ballet movies, I thought—And I got my hair cut and all these new clothes. . . . In all modesty, I've become an extremely alluring person."

I couldn't stop sneezing. Some of the kids trying to study began to give me dirty looks. There was a lot of loud "shushing" and one guy snarled, "Go sneeze outside, willya?" A couple of people were giggling. Darlene was watching our little love scene with intense interest.

I stood up. "Leave me alone," I said. "Just let me get out of here before I get in worse trouble." My eyes were streaming so badly I could hardly see.

"I mean, I even bought three more bottles of perfume when you didn't notice how alluring I was on Monday. I thought maybe 'Folie d'Amour' was too subtle, maybe you like real blatant stuff." She stuck her wrist in my face and said, "This is 'Tropic Nights'; it's supposed to be practically *lethal,* and

you don't even react. *Gesundheit already!* So is it
any wonder that I have to—"

I was ready to tear my eyes out. Suddenly the
sneezes were coming so fast I couldn't take a breath
between them. I was choking to death on my
sneezes.

By this time the whole library was pretty much in
an uproar. I could hear the complaints and the
"Gesundheits!" and the snickering all around us.

I turned my head away from G. G.'s wrist so I
wouldn't sneeze on it—though she deserved to be
sneezed on—and all of a sudden it hit me.

"That perfume," I gasped, knocking her hand
away. "The perfume—*what is it?*"

"Hobie! You finally noticed! Do you like it?"

"Like it? *Like it?* I'm *allergic* to it!"

"Oh, no!"

"Get away from me! Just get away from me!"

G. G. backed off, looking dismayed.

A teacher came marching toward us. With G. G.
out of sniffing range the sneezes began to slow
down, though my eyes still stung. I wiped them with
the handkerchief and they stopped tearing.

"What's going on here?" the teacher demanded.

"Allergies," I said. "I was just leaving."

I reached for my books and slid them off the
table.

Way off the table. All that sneezing must have
weakened me. My English book and my Earth
Science book squirted out of my fingers like tooth-
paste from a tube. When I grabbed for them, I

knocked my loose-leaf off the table too, and it hit the floor on end, splattering papers all over the place.

The bell rang. The teacher shook her head in irritation and walked away. Most of the kids were rushing out of the library as I stood there wondering what I had ever done to deserve G. G. Graffman and this misery. I wanted to crawl under the library rug and stay there; with luck, no one would ever connect my disappearance with the lump in the library floor.

Darlene hadn't left yet. She was brushing her hair. She had her little mirror out, but she was looking at me.

"I'll help you, Hobie," G. G. said. She bent down to gather up the books and papers.

"Don't help me! Haven't you done enough?"

But G. G. was already scooping up loose-leaf pages. Suddenly she jumped up and gave a little yelp of surprise. She was looking at a piece of notebook paper. She started to smile dreamily, and when she looked up her eyes were all misty and romantic.

"Ohh, Hobie! You wrote a poem for me!"

"NO!" This was the worst—more than any normal guy could be expected to live through. Even Mac Detroit would lose his cool if this happened to him.

I lunged for G. G. "No I didn't! Give me that!"

She held it away from me. "No, it's beautiful. I want to keep it."

I grabbed the poem. And sneezed. She backed away, looking confused. "But, Hobie, it's *good*. I never knew you—"

"It's not for you!" Darlene was staring at us, fascinated, her violet eyes fixed on my red, bulging ones.

I glanced at the poem. It was the good one, the almost perfect one.

I grabbed all my books, and before I could stop myself, as if I was being driven by some mysterious unknown force, I lurched toward Darlene.

"It's for *you*," I said hoarsely, and dropped it on the table in front of her.

In the moment before I hurtled past G. G. toward the library doors, I noticed that Darlene's mouth was open in surprise, her lips like ripe—

Oh, forget it.

❦ 9 ❦

"FIERY FISTS OF DEATH IS STILL PLAYING AT THE mall," Nate said. "You want to go Saturday?"

"Sure," I said. "I'm in the mood for killing and maiming."

"Come on, Hobie. Things didn't work out so bad. Darlene liked your poem, didn't she?"

"I guess so," I admitted.

"I know so."

He did. The day after G. G.'s killer perfume attack, Darlene stopped me as I walked by her desk in English class. "I liked your poem, Hobie," she said.

Naturally Nate heard her. He didn't even laugh too hard as I stumbled past him to my desk.

"And G. G. hasn't been hitting on you," Nate pointed out.

"She'd better not. She's the one I feel like killing and maiming." Boy, did I have plans for G. G. if she ever came near me again. *Terminate with Extreme*

Pain had a number of truly creative methods for dealing with your enemies. I wanted to try all of them on G. G.

"She did you a favor," Nate said. "You might never have given Darlene that poem if it wasn't for G. G."

"I would've when I was ready. And at least nobody but Darlene would have known about it."

"Except Shawna Shepherd and Lesley Parker and two hundred of their most intimate friends," Nate said. "And you'd never have been ready."

Nate might have had a point—especially if I waited until I pressed fifty pounds. I hadn't worked out with weights for a week—not since G. G. trapped me in the library.

Why bother? Darlene had the poem; if I was going to score points with her for my romantic nature, I ought to follow up with personal contact, fast. If I waited until I got my biceps to bulge she might forget I'd ever written her a poem.

Nate was right. I never did seem to be ready. But if Darlene was interested, why didn't *she* call *me?* Girls do that all the time.

Even though she said she liked the poem, that didn't mean she liked the poet. She was probably still laughing at me and my sneezing and my completely uncool way of handling G. G.'s advances.

And my father was disappointed in me again. When I stopped working out he said, "This time I really thought you were going to set a goal and reach it." He started asking me about school. He started talking about college. It was like he'd forgotten everything he'd read in *How to Talk to Your Teenager*.

And I got a 60 on the Earth Science make-up quiz.

Oh, yeah, I had a lot of reasons for wanting to terminate G. G., with extreme pain, and it was a good thing for her she was steering clear of me. Nate said she was probably embarrassed by what had happened, and was afraid to face me.

"She ought to be afraid to face me," I snarled. "Because if she does, she's not gonna have a face." Don Vitello Tonnato said that; I couldn't have put it better.

Saturday afternoon I worked at the bookstore. Nate was going to meet me after work and we'd get something to eat and go to see *Fiery Fists of Death*. Since Wednesday afternoon, my grandfather had been watching me like he was studying me for a test. He knew there was something wrong, but he wasn't going to push me into telling him.

A couple of times on Saturday he asked me to come into the back and help him with some returns and inventory work, like he wanted to give me every chance to open up.

But somehow I couldn't. I'd talked to him plenty of times when things bothered me, like my father's moods, but this was a different kind of problem and I wasn't sure he'd understand. Even if he did, it couldn't seem very important to him. I was a teenager and he was seventy. He'd think the whole thing was silly—like something you'd see on *Love Boat*.

About four o'clock there was a lull in Bookathon.

One guy was looking through the Chilton auto repair manuals, going through so many of them that he must have had twelve broken cars strewn around his back yard. Another customer was browsing the Sci Fi section, and that was it.

Jennifer was on her break and my grandfather was in the back phoning in an order. I was chomping on a piece of gum and deciding whether or not to reread an early Mac Detroit book, when Darlene walked in.

She strolled over to me and leaned her elbows on the counter like she had all the time in the world.

"Hi, Hobie." Her voice was sort of breathy, like G. G.'s when she tried to sound like a *Cosmo* girl. Only Darlene really sounded like one.

I swallowed my gum. "Hi."

"You're working late today." She tossed her hair back.

"Can't fool you for a minute," I said weakly. Then I worried that I sounded too sarcastic, but I didn't have to worry. She never noticed.

She gazed at me, her violet eyes solemn, till I had to grab the edge of the counter to keep from grabbing *her*.

"Do you have to work tonight too?" she asked.

"Uh, no. I mean, just till seven. Then I'm going to the movies." This is your chance, Katz! She's alone, she didn't come in here to buy a book, she asked what you're doing tonight. How much more obvious can she be?

Ask her! Ask her to meet you at the movies. The poem worked. Now, *do* something!

74

The guy who was looking through the Chiltons came up to the counter with his manuals. I shot him such a look of hate he must have wondered if I was crazy. I must have been. He was about five-eleven and built like a tank.

"Cash or charge?" I growled. He almost bolted.

"Cash," he said timidly.

I was afraid Darlene would disappear. I was afraid I had dreamed her here in the first place. I just couldn't believe it was happening, and I was sure the minute I looked down to punch the cash register, she'd be gone.

But she wasn't. She moved off to the side a little and played with strands of her hair like new-mown wheat until the guy took his bookbag and hurried out.

Then she turned back to me. "What movie are you going to?"

I almost started to tell her, when I remembered that she'd seen *Fiery Fists of Death* last week. With Warren. Stay cool, I told myself. Play it cagey.

"I haven't decided yet. Are you going to the movies too?"

It came out a lot cooler than I felt. In fact, I felt so un-cool I thought my ankles were sweating. This is a very strange feeling. I'd never known ankles could sweat.

"Yeah. I'm going to see *Wild Bill*."

"*Wild Bill?* What is that, a cowboy movie?" You're doing fine, Katz. Cool as a cucumber. Keep up the good work. Hold onto the edge of the counter.

"It's about Bill Welter and how he started a labor union." She wrinkled her nose. She looked adorable with her nose wrinkled. "It's a project for History."

"Actually, that sounds kind of interesting. After all"—I pointed to my chest—"I'm labor, you know. Ho ho."

I sounded smooth. Suave, almost. Well, maybe semi-suave. I wondered how I was doing it. All I knew was that this was my opening, the perfect opportunity. Darlene had even set it up for me. All I had to do was say, "Hey, why don't we meet in front of the movies—say, ten to eight?" Couldn't have been easier.

I could almost hear Mac Detroit whispering in my ear, "Don't blow it, sucker," when Darlene lowered her long, black eyelashes and said, "Did you really write that poem for me, Hobie?"

Maybe it was the eyelashes, but all I could do was gulp and nod.

"Do you think you could write me another one?" she asked, almost shyly.

Holy cow. Katz, I told myself, hard as it is to believe, you have this girl wrapped around your little finger. She has really fallen for you and your romanticness. She probably realizes that compared to you Warren Adler is an insensitive lunk. She's even shy with you—and Darlene DeVries has never been known for her introverted, retiring personality.

Bookathon seemed to take on a rosy, shimmery glow, that started from Darlene and spread around the whole store. Everything was hushed, almost like we were hanging in suspension: me, Darlene, the one customer left, the books. Like time had stopped and the only thing that would get it started again was my answer to Darlene.

I suddenly felt very powerful—and very confident.

I put my hands on the counter and leaned toward her. "Darlene," I said solemnly, "writing poems is not easy. A poet needs *inspiration*. Those lines came from my heart. I looked at you from afar, and that was what I felt. I'd love to write you another poem, Darlene. *Inspire me*."

Where was I getting this stuff? Not from Mac Detroit.

Darlene exhaled softly. I could have knocked her over with a feather. I could have knocked *me* over with a feather. The girl was hopelessly smitten.

"Hobie? Do you think maybe you could meet me at the movies tonight? I mean, if you really want to see *Wild Bill*."

"I want to see you," I said. "Be there at ten to eight." This was fantastic. This was killer magnetism. I had her mesmerized.

"Okay." She looked a little dubious. "But the movie starts at seven-forty-five."

It was only a momentary setback. "Check. Seven-thirty then."

"Will you give me the poem tonight?"

"Darlene," I said patiently, "I told you. Great art is not like making chopped liver. It takes time. And first you have to inspire me."

"Ohh." She seemed very impressed.

I know I was.

Darlene left and I breathed out—for what seemed like the first time in fifteen minutes. Bookathon came alive again. Customers were suddenly strolling around the racks, my grandfather emerged from the back room, Jennifer returned from her break.

The feeling of suspension was gone. I'd told Darlene I would write her another poem, and time started up again.

Jennifer took one look at me and grinned. "You look extremely self-satisfied. Was that Darlene I just passed?"

"I am and it was," I said smugly.

"Let me guess. She discovered that you have it. Whatever 'it' is."

"Yeah," I said. "But you know what's even better? *I* discovered that I have it."

❧ 10 ❧

AFTER FOUR FOOT-LONG HOT DOGS AT FRANKS A Lot, Nate and I ambled through the mall toward the Multiplex. I checked my watch. Again.

"Okay, Hobie, what is it? Something's up. You've been looking at your watch every two minutes and I haven't seen you looking this happy since you cheated me out of my Lou Pinella baseball card."

"Holy cow, Nate, you still remember that? We were ten years old. And I didn't cheat you out of it. I won it."

"By cheating. Anyway, what's going on?"

I cleared my throat nervously. "You know how we planned to see *Fiery Fists of Death?*"

Nate whirled around and stopped in the middle of the mall. "What do you mean, *planned?*" He crossed his hands over his chest. *"What do you mean, planned?"*

"Nate, you're going to be really excited about

79

this." I made myself sound a lot more confident than I felt. "I mean, you're my best friend, and I know that what you want most is for me to be happy."

"Not if it means I'm gonna be *un*happy."

"Darlene practically begged me to go to the movies with her," I said. "Practically *begged* me. Can you picture that, Nate? Me and *Darlene DeVries?*"

Suddenly Nate didn't look dangerous anymore. He broke into a big, broad smile and punched me in the shoulder. "Hey, hey, Horrible Hobie wins the big one! Way to go, buddy. *Way to go!*"

"Thanks," I said modestly. "But the thing is, she has to see *Wild Bill*. It's a school assignment or something. So I can't see *Fiery Fists of Death* with you. I mean, I hate to let you down, but you know how it is."

"Sure, man, sure, don't worry about it. That's the movie about the labor unions, right?"

"How did you know?"

"I saw a commercial. It might be pretty good. They had lots of violence back in those early days."

"You mean you want to *see* it?" I asked.

"Why not? Besides, I'll get a chance to watch you in action. Maybe I can learn something." He leered.

I discovered I felt a little strange about having Nate hang around while I was exercising my killer charm on Darlene. The thing was, I wasn't sure I could exercise it with Nate watching. I'd keep waiting for him to snicker.

It wasn't only that. It was, this was supposed to

be just between Darlene and me. It wasn't supposed to be a threesome. Nate and I had been friends for seven years, and for seven years we did almost everything together.

But tonight I wanted to be with Darlene more than I wanted to be with Nate. I wanted to hold her hand. Maybe even put my arm around her. Maybe even—if I worked up the nerve—kiss her. And I didn't want Nate calling a play-by-play of my moves.

My eyes were already searching out Darlene, even though we had about ten more stores to pass before we got to the Multiplex. I was trying to think of something to say that would persuade Nate not to tag along with Darlene and me, but I couldn't think of anything that wouldn't hurt his feelings.

Finally I said, "Hey, Nate, you can see *Fiery Fists of Death* if you want. You don't have to go to the other one just because we're going."

It sounded weird to say "we" and not be talking about Nate and me.

"And let my good buddy down? No way," Nate said. "I'll be sitting right behind you, in case you need me."

Need you for *what?* I wanted to ask. Darlene's hand wasn't so heavy that I couldn't hold it myself.

"Hey! There she is, sports fans! All suited up and ready to play!"

I groaned. Nate was starting already. What in the world would he say when—if—I tried to kiss her?

But she was there, and for a moment I forgot

about Nate. She was wearing her gray suede jacket and black pants and a sweater that seemed, from a distance, to be violet—the same color as her eyes.

Suddenly I was glad Nate was with me. At least for now. Because my heart actually stopped beating just before it did a nosedive down to my gut—which was a block of ice.

I clutched at Nate's arm. I couldn't breathe.

"Nate," I said hoarsely. "Nate."

"Don't choke, Horrible Hobe," he muttered. "Don't choke. The hometown fans are depending on you."

Darlene started toward us. I couldn't move. Nate shook my hand off his arm.

"Hi, Hobie. Hi, Nate," Darlene said. She didn't seem too upset or surprised that Nate was with me. I thought that was sort of odd, because I certainly would have been disturbed if she'd brought Shawna and Lesley along.

"Hello, Darlene," Nate said. "You're looking splendid this evening." He kicked me gently in the ankle, sort of the way you nudge a horse to get him moving.

"Thank you." Then, using her husky voice, Darlene said, "Do *you* think I look splendid, Hobie?"

Splendid wasn't the right word. I wasn't sure what the right word was for the way she looked, or if there was any word at all for the way she made me feel.

"Splendid." I nodded. Then I just breathed for a while.

We stood on the ticket line, and when we got to the window I said, "Three for *Wild Bill*."

"Hobie, you don't have to pay for my ticket," Darlene said. "I didn't mean for you to—"

"That's all right," I said, as the woman punched out three tickets. "I want to."

"That's very nice of you," Darlene said.

"It sure is," Nate agreed. "Thanks, sport."

I looked sideways at him. He was grinning from ear to ear. I'd never meant to pay for Nate, but what could I do? I didn't want to look cheap in front of Darlene, so I just sighed and forked over the money for three tickets.

Inside Movie Four I hesitantly put my hand on the back of Darlene's shoulder to sort of guide her down the aisle as we looked for seats. She didn't punch me in the mouth, so I increased the pressure a little, steering her to a row where there were two seats together on the aisle. The theater wasn't too full, so there was really no way I could ditch Nate. Wherever we sat he could get a seat right behind us.

But he didn't. He took a seat two rows away, as if he knew I wanted my privacy.

Of course, he'd still be able to see everything that went on between Darlene and me. I hoped two tall people would come in soon and take the seats behind us.

Darlene and I sat down and I suddenly realized that we hadn't bought any popcorn or anything. I smacked my forehead at my stupidity.

"What's the matter, Hobie?"

Suave, I told myself. Cool. Remember how you were this afternoon. Don't blow the image.

"I was so—um—enchanted with you, Darlene, I completely forgot about the more ordinary things in life. Like popcorn. I guess it's true what they say. When you're—uh—involved with someone you really do lose your appetite. Would you like some popcorn?"

"Oh, yes. Get the big box. And some Good 'n' Plenty."

I thought about this for a minute. "Well, maybe it's more true for some people than for others."

I got the popcorn and the Good 'n' Plenty and Darlene started crunching and chewing as the lights went down. She ate most of the popcorn and all of the Good 'n' Plenty. I really didn't have much interest in food.

As soon as she finished the last of the popcorn I made my move. Maybe my self-confidence was building up because Darlene hadn't punched me in the mouth when I helped her to her seat. I suspected that if I tried to hold her hand, she wouldn't punch me in the mouth this time either.

I slid my arm across hers on the armrest and gently laced our fingers together. I guess they were still a little slippery from the artificial butter; they didn't mesh right. I had two fingers left over. Darlene didn't seem to mind—in fact, she hardly seemed to notice that I was holding her hand—but it bothered me. I readjusted my fingers until they were all evenly separated by her fingers.

She didn't punch me in the mouth.

I shifted in my seat a little and savored the feeling of Darlene DeVries' hand in mine. It was warm, and a little sticky and sort of limp. It just kind of lay there in mine on the edge of the armrest. I sneaked a peek at her from the corner of my eye. She was looking straight ahead at the screen, as though she was totally unaware of anything but the movie; as if her hand wasn't connected to her body at all.

I squeezed it, gently. She squeezed back. A little. She still had her eyes fixed on the movie, as though her hand's response was sort of an automatic reflex.

Reflex or not, I felt a definite jump in my pulse rate. I squeezed her hand again. Harder. She squeezed back. A little.

We sat there for a while, holding hands. I didn't want to overdo the squeezing bit; I was afraid it might show a lack of imagination. I wondered about Darlene's pulse rate. I slid my thumb out from under hers and stroked her wrist a little. I wasn't aiming for originality, I was aiming for her pulse. I couldn't find it. I nearly dislocated my thumb trying.

My hand was beginning to get damp. Or maybe it was her hand. I wasn't sure. The initial thrill of twining fingers with Darlene DeVries was starting to wear off. I began to want a bigger thrill.

I figured that the next step was to put my arm around her, but the strategy stumped me. Ideally the movement should be smooth, natural, flowing logically from the hand-holding. But how could I put my arm around her without letting go of her hand and breaking the mood?

It was getting awfully warm in the theater. My ankles were sweating again. Wild Bill had nearly all of San Francisco shut down in a general strike before I remembered I had *two* hands.

I put my left hand over hers, so that her hand was clasped in both of mine, then slid my right hand free and draped it over the back of her seat. A riot broke out on the San Francisco docks, and in the confusion, I let my arm drop around her shoulders and pulled her toward me a little.

I held my breath, waiting for her to punch me in the mouth, or maybe pull away from me. My heart was doing a tap dance in my chest and my Adam's apple felt funny.

She didn't punch me in the mouth.

She gave a little sigh and bent her head toward me. Quick as a flash, I bent my head so my cheek rested against her hair. It felt like silk and smelled of flowers and I hoped I wasn't allergic to her perfume because if I started to sneeze now I would kill myself.

I kept my hand firmly on her upper arm which, unfortunately, was still in the sleeve of her suede jacket because she'd never taken it off, but I could still feel her arm through it and smell the flowers in her hair and if I turned my head thirty degrees I could kiss her on the eyebrow.

I don't remember anything about the rest of the movie.

As we walked up the aisle toward the exit, I looked around for Nate. He wasn't in his seat and I didn't see him in the bunch of people heading for the doors. Maybe he'd gotten bored with the movie, or with waiting for Darlene and me to put on our sideshow. It *had* taken me almost an hour to get my arm around her.

Darlene let me buy her a pink bubble-gum ice cream cone at Baskin-Robbins, and I began to wonder about getting her home. I could call my mother to drive us—but that would mean she'd be sitting in the car, watching me walk Darlene to her front door.

I had a definite need to taste Darlene's pink bubble-gum lips, even if only for a quick goodnight kiss. I'd pictured this scene many times; my mother was never in the picture.

Or Darlene could call her mother. That would be even worse. They'd drive me home and Darlene wouldn't walk me to *my* door. And how could I kiss her in the car with her mother spying on us through the rearview mirror?

What was I going to do? I couldn't get a driver's license for another two years. I couldn't *wait* two years to kiss Darlene. What did Mac Detroit do for romance when he was fourteen?

Probably stole a car.

Darlene swirled the tip of her little pink tongue around her ice cream and captured a little pink bubble-gum chip. I gulped down half a scoop of Rocky Road and the pain that bounced from my teeth and clanged to my head distracted me from Darlene's little pink tongue. And none too soon.

Along with the blinding flash of pain came a blinding flash of inspiration. Grandpa. He was probably closing up at this very moment. He could drive us home. Darlene's house was a little out of his way, but he wouldn't mind. I could tell him not to park right in front when he waited for me; he wouldn't mind that either.

"Come on, Darlene." I grabbed her hand and pulled. "My grandfather can drive us home."

"Okay." She sounded only mildly interested. She was obviously unaware that there had been a transportation problem at all. She certainly didn't realize the implications of my solution.

We made it to Bookathon one minute before my grandfather and Jennifer closed the store. I introduced Darlene to them and Grandpa seemed delighted at the prospect of chauffering us. I was afraid he'd wink, but he didn't.

Darlene and I sat very properly and kind of far apart in the backseat of the car. I don't even trust my grandfather with a rearview mirror. We made some small talk with him about the movie. Darlene did most of the talking. She remembered a lot more of it than I did.

When we got to Darlene's house I helped her out of the car, then leaned my head back in to whisper to Grandpa. "Would you park around the corner? I'll only be a minute."

"Take as long as you want. I'm in no rush." He grinned knowingly. He didn't wink, but Santa Claus could have taken twinkling lessons from him.

He drove toward the corner. I put my arm around Darlene's waist and felt our hips bump as we walked up to her door. There was a floodlamp over the garage, bright enough to light a night baseball game in her driveway. There were lanterns on each side of her front door, too. Not as bright as the floodlight, but you'd have no trouble reading a telephone book under them.

We walked up the steps to the front door.

You could have cut the tension with a knife.

Do I kiss her now? Here? Do I just grab her, or do I ask "May I?" Should I growl, "C'mere, baby," in my Bogart voice and bend her backwards in my arms?

What if I drop her right on her head?

Should I put my hands on her shoulders, close my eyes, and peck her gently on the lips? What if I missed her mouth entirely and kissed her on the eyeball?

Actually, I think the only nerves that were jangling were mine. I felt like a rubber band ready to snap, but Darlene seemed pretty calm.

"Thank you for a lovely evening," she said. "I really never meant for you to pay for me."

"You're worth it," I said hoarsely. "I mean—you're worth far more, Darlene. *Far* more."

"Did I inspire you enough?" she asked.

You have no idea. And then, suddenly, it was easy.

"Almost." I made my voice heavy with meaning. I put my hands on her shoulders and looked into her eyes, trying to make my gaze penetrating, mesmerizing. "Almost . . ."

She closed her eyes and lifted her chin and I ducked my head and kissed her right on the lips. It was a very short kiss because I felt like the breath had been knocked out of me. But it was long enough to taste bubble gum and popcorn and lipstick and to make me so dizzy that I slid my arms around her and held her against me almost for support as I kissed her again.

"Darlene . . ."

"Now can you write the poem?" She looked up at me with big, hopeful eyes.

"I'll shower you with poems," I promised. I was surprised that my voice sounded normal. I was surprised I had a voice at all. "I'll *deluge* you with poems. I'll go home and write one right now. Before the inspiration wears off."

My legs were spaghetti as I walked down the front steps, hanging onto the wrought iron railing.

But by the time I reached the corner there was a definite spring in my step, and I probably looked pretty jaunty when I gave Grandpa the thumbs-up sign.

❧11❧

Sweet are the lips that I kissed tonight,
Sweeter than roses or wine,
Sweet are the dreams I will dream tonight,
Now that I know you are mine.

I WAS GETTING REALLY GOOD AT THIS. SO GOOD IT
was almost scary. I tossed that one off two minutes
after I got home Saturday night and woke up Sunday morning with another opening line in my head.

I called Nate to find out why he'd disappeared
after the movie.

"Katz, you are so *boring*. I mean, I was really
ashamed for the home team. I sat there for half an
hour before I sneaked into *Fiery Fists of Death*. At
least that had some action."

"Hey, listen, man. You should have sat there a
little bit longer. The game isn't over until the fat
lady sings."

"Yeah? So what happened?"

"Come on over. I'll tell you the whole thing. You might need some pointers some day."

"Well, I'll tell you, Hobe. Not today. I'm—uh—I have to get some help with the geometry home-work."

"You got a tutor?"

"Not exactly," Nate said. His voice sounded kind of funny—secretive or something. "I ran into G. G. after the movie last night and happened to mention—"

"G. G.?" I cackled. "You're letting G. G. help you with geometry?"

"She's very good in math," Nate said indignantly.

"Well, hey, that's great," I said. "Let her make *you* crazy. Anything to keep her away from me. I'm going to be real busy with Darlene. I mean, *real* busy . . . if you catch my drift." I hoped he noticed the leer in my voice.

"That's great, Hobe." He sounded sort of dis-tracted. "Listen. Have you gotten a good look at her lately?"

"A good look isn't all I've gotten, my man."

"No, I meant at G. G. She's not a bad kid."

"I don't believe this!" I cried. "G. G. Graffman? You actually like—"

"Forget it, Hobe. You're prejudiced. Besides, she's only helping me with geometry. Talk to you later."

When I was finally able to stop laughing I realized that this was a very convenient turn of events. I mean, I didn't believe for a minute that Nate was seeing G. G. just to get help in math.

It was a good thing that G. G. hadn't been so crushed by my rejection that she stopped blooming altogether and went back into her shellfish. It was a relief to know that she would now be blooming on Nate, leaving me free to concentrate on the only budding romance I wanted in my life.

It was amazing how quickly girls got over broken hearts. G. G. was able to control her passion for me in a week and Darlene had stopped chasing Warren Adler after reading one four-line poem.

Darlene . . .
Darling . . .

I stopped at Darlene's desk in English class on Monday.

"I wrote you another poem," I whispered. I reached into my notebook and she got sort of a nervous look in her eyes and grabbed hold of my wrist.

"Not here," she whispered. "I want to read it in private. I want you to give it to me some place where we can be *alone.*"

For a moment the room tilted and the edges of Darlene's desk looked wavy as the full impact of what she was saying hit me.

The girl is so overwhelmed by her emotions she's afraid she'll do something really uncool when she reads the poem. Like cry, or throw her arms around me with unrestrainable passion. Naturally she doesn't want to lose control of herself in front of the whole class.

"The bookstore," I said. "Be there by five." I patted her hand affectionately. I hoped that would hold her till later.

I rolled my eyes as I walked past Nate's desk. He flashed me a gentle smile, but he didn't seem to be too interested in my love life.

He must have gotten a lot of help with geometry.

It was quiet, as it usually is in the late afternoon when Darlene came into the store. I didn't think I was imagining that she seemed a little hesitant, a little nervous as she approached the counter. Funny how the more nervous she looked, the less nervous I felt.

"I've been counting the hours till you came," I said. I tried my mesmerizing gaze on her.

"It's only four-thirty," she said.

"It feels like an eternity. Come on in the back. We can be alone there."

I grabbed my notebook and she followed me to the back room, where my grandfather grasped the situation in an instant and went to straighten out the magazine racks.

I pulled the poem out of my notebook and handed it to her. I watched her as she read it, a little wrinkle of concentration between her eyebrows, her adorable lips forming the words like she was tasting them.

When she looked up from the page, her eyes were shining.

"Oh, Hobie, this is wonderful. This is *perfect*."

"Only because my inspiration was perfect," I said. "Without you there'd be no poem."

Was there no end to my suaveness? My voice was so smooth you could have skated on it. Any day now Mac Detroit would be stealing his lines from me.

Darlene lowered her eyes and looked almost modest. "What a nice thing to say."

"I have a way with words."

She blinked her long, beautiful eyelashes a few times. She really *is* moved, I thought. She might be struggling not to cry.

"Now—" I took the poem from her hand and dropped it on the desk. I pulled her arms around my waist. "You do something nice for me."

She tilted her head and kissed me lightly on the lips.

"That's a start." I threw my arms around her and kissed her passionately. I was even ready to try bending her backwards over the desk, but it was littered with order forms and catalogues and bills and staplers, so I thought better of it.

When I let go of her she was breathless. I could taste her lipstick on my mouth.

"Sit down." I pointed to a carton of books. I was afraid she might faint from the raging torrent of emotions I was stirring in her.

"I have to meet my mother in a few minutes."

"Well, maybe I'll sit down then," I said weakly. I perched on a carton of *Eternal Embers*.

"Where did you learn to kiss like that, Hobie?"

She used her husky-sexy voice, and I thought some-body would have to apply cold compresses to me in a minute.

I cleared my throat. "I guess poetry isn't the only thing you inspire in me, Darlene." Poetry was hardly what I had on my mind. I wasn't feeling poetic at all; what I was feeling mainly was that I had too many glands, all of which were working overtime.

I wondered how I could go about kissing her on the neck. In the movies women go crazy when you kiss them on the neck. I stood up and began to try to work out an approach, taking into account our relative heights and her suede jacket, which she was wearing with the collar up.

"Am I inspiring you now?" she asked.

"Oh, yes. My brain is churning with possibili-ties."

"For a poem?"

"Among other things." I eyed her neck. Her sweater came up to her chin. I wasn't sure that kissing her neck through a layer of polyester would make her go crazy.

"Will you write me another one?"

"Another what?" I think my mind was wandering a little away from her neck.

"Another poem." She sounded almost irritable. "Another beautiful poem," she added.

Holy cow, the girl was insatiable. Check this out, Mac Detroit. The pen is mightier than the .357 Magnum.

"C'mere and inspire me some more." My low

growl would have frightened off most girls, but Darlene was hopelessly hooked. Even so, she hesitated before she sat down next to me on the carton.

"Your grandfather—"

"Will stay out front." I put my arm around her shoulder and hugged her against me.

"My mother—"

"Won't leave the Mall without you." I kissed her just under the jaw, which was the closest I could get to her neck without running into man-made fibers. She gave a little sigh and settled against me. I guess the jaw was close enough.

I kissed the corner of her mouth, then turned her head toward me. Another long, lingering kiss on the lips and she melted in my arms. At least, I think she did. One of us melted. It may have been me.

She stood up. I guess she was too overcome by flaming desire to trust herself with me any longer. "I really have to go, Hobie. I hope I inspired you enough."

"We've already established that, Darlene." I got to my feet. My hormones felt like they were celebrating New Year's Eve in Times Square. "The question is, do *I* inspire *you?*"

"What?" She seemed bewildered.

"Never mind." It occurred to me that Darlene might not actually know the meaning of the word "inspired," in which case she should have consulted a dictionary long before this. It occurred to me that I didn't care if she knew what "inspired" meant, as long as she *was*.

"I really have to go now," Darlene said. "When do you think you'll write me another poem?"

"I don't know, Darlene. It depends on my muse." If she didn't know what "inspire" meant, "muse" was certainly going to throw her, but that was okay. Let her think I was a little mysterious. Women love mystery men. They think we're a challenge.

"I'm here Monday, Wednesday, and Friday," I went on. "Why don't you come in day after tomorrow?"

"Okay."

"Hey, don't forget this." I leaned over and handed her the poem I'd tossed on the desk.

"Oh, I'll never forget this, Hobie." She folded it up and tucked it into her purse. "When you're a famous poet I'll show it to people."

She smiled beautifully, put her fingers to her lips and kissed them. She puckered her mouth and blew the kiss toward me. I lunged for her, but she dodged out into the store before I could grab her delicate pink-tipped fingers, on which I suddenly had a wild, irresistible urge to nibble.

My father was reading *Set Fire to Your Staff* when I got home. At first I thought it was something biblical, but it turned out to be a book on how to inspire your sales force to achieve their full potential. He had either finished *How to Talk to Your Teenager* or given up on it.

"Want to work out a little before dinner?" I asked

tentatively. I wasn't sure if he'd given up on me, along with the book.

"Sure! Great!" he said. "I didn't think you were going to—" He stopped himself, like he had to swallow the words. Maybe he had finished the book.

He tossed *Set Fire to Your Staff* aside without even marking his place. "I've got a lot of tension to work off," he said.

"Me too."

"Tension? At your age? Is something bothering you?"

He looked so concerned that I said, "No, no, there's nothing bothering me," until he believed me. "Maybe tension isn't exactly the right word," I added.

But it would have to do—at least till my father read a book called *How to Listen to Your Teenager*.

❧ 12 ❧

Our love is like a flower that blooms,
To brighten up the darkest rooms.
I'll tell you in poetry or in prose,
My heart will follow wherever yours goes.

DARLENE WAS REALLY PUTTING THE PRESSURE ON.
I guess I struck an unconscious chord in her, tapped
this hidden spring of literary appreciation that she
never knew she had. The girl was crazy for poetry.

I thought about giving her a book of poems from
the store to stave her off for a while, but I realized
that she probably didn't want to read love poems
written to somebody else. I suspected that
Darlene's voracious appetite for verse could only
be satisfied by verse about Darlene.

I wrote poems every night. Or tried to. I tore up a
lot. That first burst of inspiration had died down; for
poems, I mean, not for Darlene. They were coming

slower now and I was getting more critical. I only gave her the "My heart will follow" one out of desperation.

But she liked it well enough. She showed me a lot of literary appreciation after I gave it to her in the back room at Bookathon.

The poems, plus my homework, plus working in the store and working out at home three days a week, (the days Darlene came to Bookathon) left me hardly any time for anything else. Or any*one* else. I hadn't talked to Nate in almost a week.

So I was really glad to see him when he came into the store Friday afternoon, even though it was pretty busy and I was trying to write a poem in between waiting on customers. Even though I was wondering how I could manage some time alone in the back with Darlene and wondering how I could manage if I *didn't* get some time alone with her.

Even though Nate had G. G. with him.

"Hey, Nate!" I yelled, over the head of a middle-aged guy buying *New Wave Needlepoint*. "Good to see you!"

"Hi, Hobe. Pretty busy, huh?"

G. G. greeted me calmly, as if she had never attacked me with her killer perfume, never tried to make me crazy, hardly even knew me.

Just as well, I thought. Allergies, keep your distance.

"Never too busy for a friend!" I said cheerily. Several of the customers in line glared at me. My grandfather came up front to help and that stifled a few snarls.

"Talk to you later," Nate said. "We're going to get a book."

"We." Nate had said "We," as in Nate & G. G. This was really getting serious. I put *New Wave Needlepoint* in a bag, and watched the back of G. G.'s head as she and Nate disappeared down the Science and Technology aisle. Her new haircut really was an improvement.

I stapled the receipt to the bag and said my automatic "Have a nice day." I couldn't see G. G. now, but her image had made a definite impression on my brain. She'd gotten herself a suede jacket, something like Darlene's, only in dark green. She wore black slacks, short black boots, and a black turtleneck sweater with some gold chains. Actually, she looked sort of . . . well, almost sophisticated. I wondered if Nate had ever kissed her on the neck.

I wondered if Nate had ever kissed her at all.

I wondered why I was wondering this.

I charged the next person on the line $103 for a *TV Guide*.

I concentrated on the customers after that, until I saw Nate at the end of the line. G. G. didn't wait on line with him. She went over the magazine racks and made a big show of examining them. I know she was making a big show of it, because she was careful to keep her back to me.

When Nate reached the register I glanced at the book he'd chosen. *The ABC's of Algae*. "Buying G. G. a present?"

Nate said "Hi" to my grandfather and then shook his head. "No. It's for me."

I thought I'd die laughing. I thought I ought to point out to Nate how hard I was trying not to die laughing. "See how I'm keeping a straight face?" I hardly moved my lips. "See how I'm not saying a word about the Princess of Plankton?"

Nate smiled tolerantly. "Yeah. I really appreciate that. Keep up the good work."

"You too." I rolled my eyes. "But seriously, folks, how about a movie tonight?"

"Sorry. Hobe. G. G. and I are—"

"Don't say another word. I understand." I rang up Nate's book and put it in a bag. "At least, I think I do." But I shrugged elaborately as if the whole thing mystified me.

My heart wasn't entirely in it, though. G. G. may have been a late bloomer, but her blossoms weren't in bad shape and she seemed cooler and more confident now. She hadn't acted dippy or flustered when she saw me. That must have taken a lot of poise.

Nate said something vague about getting together on Sunday, and then he and G. G. left the store. They were holding hands as they walked out. G. G.'s new slacks seemed to fit very nicely.

Darlene didn't come in till five forty-five. By that time I was getting really nervous wondering if she'd show up at all, but at least Jennifer had arrived and business had slowed down enough so that Grandpa didn't need me up front for a while.

As soon as we were alone in the back room I gave Darlene a welcoming kiss that took her breath away. She practically went limp in my arms, but she did manage to choke out a few words as she pulled away from me. "Did you write me a poem, Hobie?"

"I'm working on one now. It's not finished yet."

"Oh." Darlene smoothed her hair back. She had a little gold heart on her earlobe. It was so cute and delicate; so was her earlobe. I was fascinated. I couldn't tear my eyes away from Darlene's ear. Would Darlene think I was crazy if I kissed her on the earlobe?

"When do you think it'll be finished?" she asked.

I touched the tiny heart with my finger. I kissed her cheek, right next to her ear. "I'm not sure. Sometimes you have to work really hard to find exactly the right words. Do you want to go to the movies with me tonight?" In the theater, sitting right next to her, I could kiss her ear as much as I wanted, and it would be perfectly natural with our heads right together. I could kiss her and put my cheek on her soft, silky hair and—

"I can't," Darlene said. "I told Shawna and Lesley I'd go with them."

"Tomorrow night," I said urgently. "How about tomorrow?"

"Well, Hobie, you know I have this problem with my mother."

"Problem? What problem?"

"I'm not allowed to go out with boys." Darlene tossed her head and her hair swooped forward and covered up her ear.

"Um, no, actually you never told me that, Darlene."

"That's one of the reasons I don't want anyone to

know about the poems. If my mother ever found out—" She made a terrible face.

I shuddered a little myself, thinking of Darlene locked up in her room, our love frustrated, our kisses kaput. I pictured myself standing forlorn, under her window, calling, "Darlene, Darlene, let down your hair," and Darlene crying, "Hobie, it's not long enough for you to climb up it yet. That'll take another six months, minimum."

"When did you say that poem would be finished?" Darlene asked.

"Darlene. *Darling*. Forget about the poem for a minute. We have a real problem here." Boy, do we have a problem. "You mean, you can never go out with me? We can never go any place together? Is that what you're telling me?"

"That's right. And that's why nobody must ever know about . . . *us*."

Us. The way she said it, soft, breathy, a little hesitant, made me wild. I kissed her face a few hundred times, till she gasped, "Hobie!" and pushed at my chest. She looked somewhat flustered, which was perfectly understandable, and her two pearly front teeth bit nervously into her lower lip.

"Why does she have to know?" I asked. "You can meet me here or anywhere, or come to my house or—"

"No! She'll find out. Someone will talk. And then I won't even be able to come *here*."

This was such a horrible prospect that I suddenly needed to sit down. I squatted on a book carton feeling helpless, hopeless. Darlene leaned against the steel shelves that lined one wall and gazed down at me. She must have felt as desperate as I did about the situation, because there was a kind of anxious, expectant expression on her face, like she was hoping I could figure out some way to get around her mother.

But I was too unglued to figure out anything. I couldn't think at all, except about how I wanted to see Darlene for more than five or ten minutes at a time. I needed to be with her, to talk to her. I wanted to walk with her, holding hands and swinging our arms up and back like little kids.

"Darlene, this is terrible."

"I know," she said sympathetically. "I think so too."

I didn't even try to hide how upset I was. I didn't care about looking cool or sounding suave. Darlene was suffering too. My killer charm was of no use now.

I stood up and walked over to her. I took her hand and curled her fingers under mine. "What are we going to do?"

"You can still write me poems and I can meet you here," she said.

"Poems! How can I think about poems now? And we can't go on meeting like this. I only get to see you for a minute, and I'm supposed to be out there working—Darlene, I'm not made of iron, you know. I have *very strong emotions.*"

"Hobie, I have to go. My mother's going to get suspicious."

"But *Darlene—*"

"I'll be fifteen in a couple of months," she said. "She might let me date then."

"I can't wait a couple of months!"

"Hobie, please, my mother's going to kill me. I'll see you Monday. Maybe you'll have the poem finished then."

"Who cares about the stupid poem?" I yelled.

She looked at me reproachfully. "I do. You know that, Hobie . . . darling."

She pulled away and darted out the door before I even had a chance to ask her to inspire me.

I flopped back down on the carton thinking how she'd called me darling and how it didn't make any difference since our love would never develop any further than the few kisses we managed to steal among the *Eternal Embers*.

The whole thing was so ironic. Darlene and me in this small, cluttered storeroom, surrounded by books with names like *Eternal Embers* and *Flaming Desire* and *Rapturous Romance* . . . The closest we would get to *Rapturous Romance* was when we sat on it.

I laughed—a short, bitter laugh—the way Mac Detroit does when he runs up against irony, which there seems to be a lot of in his business.

My grandfather leaned inside the doorway. "Everything all right?"

I shook my head.

"The course of true love never runs smoothly," he said. This did not cheer me up. "You have to expect a bump in the road now and then."

"What if they close the road for repaving?"

He thought about this for a minute, then shrugged. "I guess you have to find an alternate route."

If there was a way to detour around Darlene's mother I couldn't think of it. I worked till Bookathon closed that night, since I had nothing better to do. Nate was with G. G. and Darlene was with Shawna and Lesley, and I was all alone with Jennifer and my grandfather.

When business was slow Jennifer talked about Brent. Not only to me, but to Grandpa. I wasn't listening too closely, because I had my own problems, but enough words filtered in for me to realize that I wasn't the only one facing bumpy roads.

With one ear I listened for Grandpa to tell Jennifer that the course of true love never runs smoothly, but he just said something like "I guess some men are dreamers. My son thinks I'm unrealistic." And she said something about a book she was reading, called *How Come I Never Pick a Winner?*

But I don't remember anything else they said. I was too wrapped up in thoughts of Darlene and her heart-shaped earring and her long blonde hair and her rotten mother. I couldn't get Darlene out of my mind. I remembered everything she'd said this afternoon, every expression on her face, every kiss I gave her. I told myself that it wasn't the end of the world, that I'd see her again on Monday, that we could still meet three times a week. Maybe I could even work something out with Jennifer or Grandpa to get some more time alone with Darlene. Sure, it wasn't an ideal situation, but it wasn't like she lived in Alaska and I could only see her twice a year.

Gradually I began to realize that our case wasn't entirely hopeless. But as I realized that, I also discovered that something more was eating at me. It was tough about Darlene's mother, but I had this weird, superstitious feeling that something else wasn't quite right. I couldn't put my finger on it. I didn't even think it was anything logical, anything solid.

Just this *feeling*.

❦ 13 ❧

My heart is heavy as a stone,
We are apart and I'm alone.
I think of you with every breath.
Without your love my life is death.

MAYBE THAT WAS A LITTLE MELODRAMATIC, BUT it was how I felt. And the last line was so good it might sweep Darlene off her feet. Maybe she didn't realize how serious I felt about her. Maybe my suave technique had fooled her. She probably thought I used the same slick charm on every girl I met.

This poem would show her I meant business. It might even inspire her to ask her mother for a little slack in her leash.

Sunday afternoon I was working out in the basement. No one was at home at Nate's and my parents had gone to play tennis and if I brooded any longer about Darlene's lips like ripe fruit and hair like new-mown wheat I was going to start sucking my thumb.

Which is why I was working out in the basement when the doorbell rang. I was maybe four inches away from pressing fifty-five pounds. I was really irritated by the interruption. I tried to ignore the bell and keep lifting the barbell, but I suddenly thought maybe Darlene sneaked out of the house to see me and she'd think there was no one home and turn around and leave—

I lowered the barbell faster than I should have and nearly tore my arms out of their sockets. I pictured myself hulking around for three days with my knuckles scraping the floor. I grabbed a towel, threw it around my neck and charged upstairs. I stopped to wipe some sweat off my face and did a fast chest and underarm mop-up.

I yanked the front door open.

I guess I was more surprised than disappointed, because when I said, "Hey, G. G.!" my voice sounded kind of cheerful. I was probably just glad to have some company.

"Hi, Hobie. I thought Nate might be here."

"No, I thought he was with you." She didn't look disgusting. "Come on in. Don't stand out there in the cold."

G. G. hesitated. "Well, okay. Just for a minute. I'm not wearing any perfume."

"Ho ho," I said. "Ho ho."

She stepped inside and I closed the door behind her.

We were standing really close together. G. G.

blinked a few times, then shifted her eyes away from me, but other than that, there was no trace of the shy, fumbling, accident-prone klutz who had tried to lure me to her web.

When she didn't start babbling I began to get very conscious of the silence in the house, and how near to me she was.

"Come on in," I said. She was already in. "To the kitchen, I mean. Do you want something to eat?"

She followed me into the kitchen.

I threw open the refrigerator door and started taking inventory. "What do you want? Salami, Jell-O, hardboiled eggs, cocktail onions?"

"No thank you."

I shut the door and looked into a cabinet. "Chickpeas? Crackerjacks? Cream of celery soup?" I wondered if my mother had the kitchen alphabetized. I wondered why I was acting like such a jerk.

She perched on the edge of a chair. "I'm not hungry." She didn't even take off her jacket. Don't girls *ever* take off their coats except in school?

I leaned against the refrigerator and crossed my arms. I was aiming for nonchalant. Cordial but casual. Show her I didn't hold a grudge.

"So, you're looking for Nate?"

"Not really," G. G. said. "I mean, I thought he might be here, but we didn't make any plans. I was just taking a little walk . . ."

"Guess it's safer than falling off your bike." Right away I was sorry I said it. G. G. looked away, embarrassed, and I was embarrassed too. That was no way to show her I didn't hold a grudge. Things had worked out okay. I was going with Darlene—I guess—and G. G. had settled for Nate, and was exercising super human self-restraint.

"Listen, Hobie—" She leaned forward on the chair and brushed a wave of hair off her eyebrow.

It's like a sunset, I thought suddenly. Her hair is the color of a blazing sunset. How come I never realized that before? I used to think it was just red.

It must be this poetic nature I never knew I had until Darlene inspired me.

". . . about what happened," G. G. was saying. "I know I gave you an allergy attack in the library, and I did some other dumb things, but I embarrassed myself too. I don't know what got into me—"

She stopped herself. "Well, actually I do know, but that's not important. The important thing is, Nate's your friend, and I don't see why *we* can't be friends too. Let bygones be bygones, like they say."

"Sure," I agreed. "I know you never meant to humiliate me. You don't have to apologize. You couldn't help yourself." Any more than I could help having whatever "it" was that drove women wild.

"I'm not exactly apologizing," G. G. said. "I'm explaining. I don't want you to apologize either. I mean, I know you didn't *mean* to hurt my feelings, that you couldn't help acting like a churlish boor—"

113

"A *what?*" I knew boor, but "churlish" was a new one. Even so, I could figure it out from context.

"—that underneath that hostility was the heart of a frightened, immature—"

"Frightened?" I yelled. *"Immature? Me?"*

"Nothing personal, Hobie. Boys of your age are usually less mature than girls of my age. It's a physical fact, that's all."

"G. G., you are *barely* fourteen years old—"

"Let's face it, Hobie, you were scared of me. The simple truth is, I was just too much woman for you."

"Too much woman for me? You're crazy! That's it. You were always a little dippy, but now you're a full-grown basket case."

"If you weren't afraid of me, how come you were always running away from me?"

I was so mad I wanted to punch her. I wanted to terminate her with extreme pain. I wanted to hit her with a dumbbell. And she kept perfectly calm, practically serene. It was infuriating.

I was about to make a snappy retort to the effect that I kept running from her because I didn't want her to catch me, when I remembered what Jennifer had said about men who put women down to build themselves up. Insulting G. G. was no way to prove to her that I was mature. In fact, hurting G. G.'s feelings was suddenly something I didn't want to do. Even if I still wanted to deck her.

So I didn't say anything. Talk about superhuman self-restraint.

"I was young," G. G. said. "I matured a little."

I couldn't argue with that, no matter how angry I was.

"You will too, Hobie, in time. That's why I don't expect any apologies from you. It takes maturity to learn how to deal with the opposite sex. I'm still learning myself."

"Oh yeah? Two whole weeks of reading seduction secrets and you're not an expert yet?"

Superhuman self-restraint can go just so far.

She lowered her eyes. Now I'd really embarrassed her. I shouldn't have said it, but she deserved it. Me, immature? Me, Hobie Katz, with a passionate pen in one hand and Darlene DeVries eating out of the other?

She's jealous! I realized. That's what all this is about. G. G. had thrown herself at me, and when I wouldn't catch her she got angry. When I gave Darlene the poem in the library it pushed her over the edge.

"Hell hath no fury like a woman scorned," I muttered.

G. G. shook her head. "Look, Hobie, I'm not making boys my career. I'm just developing a side of myself that it's time to develop. It didn't work out with you, but Nate's a nice person. I didn't learn everything in two weeks; there's plenty I don't know about social interaction and personality integration."

What *was* she talking about? Probably sex.

"But I have plenty of time to learn. And lots of boys to learn from."

"You mean, there's more than one fish in the sea?" I said sarcastically.

She grinned. "You could put it that way. Pretty appropriate."

"Does Nate know he's only a minnow?" I asked. Poor Nate. G. G. was just using him to get over me, and to learn how to catch the big fish.

"Nate's not a minnow, Hobie." G. G. cocked her head to one side and looked sort of amused. "I wouldn't call Nate a minnow."

I felt myself almost drawn into the depths of her green eyes. They were flashing like emeralds. Maybe it was the light or something. Of course, her eyes always were her best feature.

I wondered if she thought I was a minnow. Suddenly I wasn't so sure that she was feeling like a woman scorned.

I was beginning to feel like a man scorned. After all, she had said some pretty scornful things to me. That stuff about me being scared and juvenile, about how she was too much woman for me was really nasty. Not to mention ridiculous.

"Nate's my friend," I said gruffly. "I just don't want him to get hurt."

"I'm going to be your friend too, Hobie, aren't I?"

This was now extremely debatable.

"I'm sure," G. G. said, "none of us wants anybody to get hurt."

"Just one thing, G. G., before we drop this whole subject forever and get to be friends. I am *not* scared of you and you are *not* too much woman for me. The thought is utterly laughable."

"All right," she said. "I could be wrong." She sounded like it didn't matter one way or the other. Like it wasn't worth arguing about.

It mattered a lot. To me.

"That poem I gave to Darlene? The one you thought was for you?" I went on. "Darlene and I have been going together ever since. And if *Darlene DeVries* isn't too much woman for me—"

I realized that now I'd told G. G. about Darlene, I'd have to swear her to secrecy. Maybe, I thought briefly, she *is* more mature than I am.

"Maybe we could all go out together sometime," G. G. said.

She stood up. The news about me and Darlene didn't seem to have any effect on her at all. The girl has iron self-control, I told myself. And then I realized it might not be a matter of self-control at all. She might actually be cured of me.

It didn't seem the right moment to tell her to keep quiet about Darlene and me. For one thing, she might think I was making it up, and when she never saw us together in school she'd be sure I'd lied just to impress her. She might even think I was jealous of her and Nate.

Nate could explain it to her, once I'd explained it to him. G. G. would know it was true if Nate told her.

I wished she would leave. I was feeling really weird. I walked to the door with her and opened it.

"Take care, Hobie. I'm glad we had this talk, aren't you?"

"Oh, yeah. It was very . . . enlightening." No it wasn't. In fact, it was very endarkening. I was more confused than ever.

G. G. slid past me as I held open the storm door. Actually she didn't manage it too smoothly; she stepped on my sneaker and her elbow missed my gut by three quarters of an inch. I sort of liked that. It was a touch of the old G. G. under this strange new layer of sophistication.

As I closed the door behind her, I realized that she hadn't used her husky *Cosmo* voice at all while she was talking to me. Either she'd given it up, or she saved it for special occasions, like when Nate kissed her ear.

I wondered if Nate ever kissed her ear.

Why was I thinking about G. G.'s ear? I hadn't even seen it; it was covered by the red sunset of her hair.

There was a poem in G. G.'s hair. Plus her eyes like deep green pools.

What was the matter with me? Darlene was my inspiration. Darlene was the one who wanted my poems. Darlene was the girl of my dreams. Hair like new-mown wheat, I reminded myself. Violet eyes. Fruity lips.

I'd have to ask Nate if he ever kissed G. G.'s ear. I mean, just to find out if I was perverted for wanting to kiss Darlene's.

Suddenly I was very hungry. I went into the kitchen and sliced up some salami. I guess it isn't true that love makes you lose your appetite. I remembered telling Darlene that the first time we went to the movies, and how she'd scarfed down popcorn and Good 'n' Plenty. Obviously you could love someone and still take normal nourishment.

I dug into the bowl of Jell-O wherever there was a piece of banana and thought how far I'd come since I first worried about how to put my arm around Darlene in the movies. No more timid fumbling with her fingers, no more wondering how to be subtle. I'd progressed to the really sophisticated stage of mapping out ear and neck kissing strategy—Darlene had even asked me where I learned to kiss.

I would never tell her I'd learned to kiss right on her front steps.

Right on her front steps.

With her mother who didn't allow her to go out with boys just inside the door. Maybe ready to open the door at any minute.

I put down the spoon.

That was it. That was what had been nagging at me Friday night in Bookathon, the sense that something more was wrong than what Darlene had told me.

If Darlene's mother was so strict, how come Darlene let me take her to the movies at all? And how could she bring me right up to her door and let me kiss her?

Even if she was understandably infatuated with me and my poetic romanticness she couldn't have been so deranged by love as to completely lose her judgment.

Could she?

This was very confusing. Confusing enough to drive all the other confusing thoughts about G. G. right out of my head.

I must have stared down into that bowl of Jell-O for ten minutes, like it was a crystal ball with the answers in it. But I couldn't come up with any answers. Plenty of bananas, but no answers. No matter how hard I tried, I couldn't think of a logical solution to this puzzle.

I'd have to call Darlene. Right now. Because if I didn't the mystery was going to drive me crazy. I didn't even worry about her mother answering the phone. I just worried about what Darlene would say to me.

Darlene's mother did answer the phone. She didn't sound outraged to hear a boy's voice asking for Darlene. She just called out, "Darlene, it's for you!"

I heard a click as Darlene picked up an extension. "I've got it!" she yelled. "Hang up." There was a gentle clunk as the other receiver was put down.

"Darlene? It's me, Hobie."

"Oh. Hi, Hobie. How are you? Did you finish the poem yet?"

She sounded perfectly normal. Not like she was worried about a boy calling her house, not like she was heartsick that we couldn't go out in public together and had no time at all in private—I guess she could have been keeping her tone natural so her mother wouldn't get suspicious.

"Yeah, I finished the poem."

"Good. I'll see you tomorrow then."

"Yeah. Listen, Darlene, there's something I want to ask you. Remember when we went to see *Wild Bill?*"

"Sure."

"How come we went to see it?"

"What do you mean?"

"Why did you go to the movies with me and let me take you home and stand right in front of your house when your mother won't let you see boys?"

There was the tiniest pause on the other end of the phone, then Darlene said, "Oh, *that* night. My parents weren't home. They went to a show in the city."

I sure wish I'd known that then. I would have told my grandfather to go on home, and Darlene and I could have been alone together—

But Darlene knew it. If her parents weren't home, why didn't she ask me to come in? If she was really deranged by love, how could she have missed the opportunity to be alone with me?

"Hobie? Are you still there?"

"I'm still here. I was just thinking. Weren't you worried that someone would see us at the movies and tell your mother?"

"Well, nobody did, so that's okay."

"Aren't you worried about me calling you? About your mother answering the phone?"

"Hobie, why are you asking me all these questions?"

"Just curious."

"Well I don't know what you're so curious about

all of a sudden," Darlene replied. "I can always tell my mother you called to get the English homework. Anyway, your voice is kind of high—she probably thought you were one of my girlfriends."

Gee, thanks. Along with everything else, I really needed that. My voice hadn't cracked for months.

"Hobie? I'll see you tomorrow, won't I?" Her voice dropped to a whispery purr. "In the store? I'll come early. I can't wait to see you."

I could almost feel vibrations from the phone as Darlene purred in my ear. It was hard to stay suspicious with my ear vibrating and my palm getting sweaty and the receiver sliding around in my hand.

Why was I cross-examining this girl? Why was I acting like a—a—churlish boor when all I wanted to do was listen to her murmur, "I can't *wait* to see you."

"I can't wait to see you either," I said. "I mean, I *really can't*. Tell your mother you're taking a walk. Come over here. Just for a little while."

"You know I can't."

No I don't. I don't know anything. I'm going nuts. I'm going to chew on the phone cord. I'm going to press fifty-five pounds. I'm going to write another poem. About your emerald eyes. I mean, your *violet* eyes! *Violet!* I'm losing my mind. I'm thinking about your neck. I'm not thinking about anything, I can't think at all—

"Hobie? Hobie?"

"Fine. Just fine." I dropped the phone.

Certified loony tune.

⤜§ 14 §⤛

Nate walked me to the Million Dollar Mall on Monday afternoon. I was really glad to be with him. There was a lot I wanted to talk about, a lot I wanted to ask him. Plus, it felt good just strolling along with old Nate again.

I'd calmed down a lot since my conversation with Darlene. But the uneasy sense of something not being right hadn't disappeared, in spite of Darlene's purring promises.

I chalked up yesterday's temporary insanity to glands, but Darlene's little secret smile to me as I'd walked by her desk in English nearly brought on a relapse. I'd be seeing her soon. Very soon. She'd promised to come early.

Kissing her, talking to her, being able to see her would clear up my confusion. That was all I needed. My suspicions—whatever they were, since I didn't know what I was suspicious of—were just paranoid.

I was imagining things and I got a little crazy when Darlene wasn't around. Sensory deprivation can make you hallucinate. Without Darlene in my arms I was definitely suffering from sensory deprivation.

"How's it going with Darlene?" Nate asked.

"Great, great. I'm meeting her at the store today. How's it going with G. G.? She came over to my house looking for you yesterday. I guess she's really hooked on you." I jabbed him in the ribs with my elbow. "You sly rascal."

Nate grinned. "She's okay."

"She didn't seem to know about me and Darlene. I thought you would have told her."

"I guess it didn't come up. To tell you the truth, we didn't talk much about you."

"I guess not. You had other fish to fry, right?"

But I was kind of surprised. I mean, I'd assumed that G. G. had first latched onto Nate because he was my friend, and maybe she would have asked him how I felt about her, what her chances were, stuff like that. And then their relationship had developed from there.

"She's a good kid," Nate said. "Smart. She can call an Islander game as well as I can."

"You like her because she understands hockey?" I asked.

"There's a better reason?"

I wondered if Nate was a little slow. I wondered if Nate was the person to ask about ear kissing. And G. G. called *me* immature.!

"Uh, Nate," I began slowly. "I want to ask you

something." Maybe I ought to work up to it. I didn't want to scare him. Hearing about sophisticated kissing before he was ready might turn him off women for life. "Did you ever kiss her?"

"Sure," he said easily. Then, suddenly, he stopped walking and turned to me with a look of surprise. "Didn't you ever kiss Darlene?"

"Of course I did! A *lot*."

He looked relieved.

"Did you like kissing G. G.?" I asked.

"What's not to like?"

He said it so casually that I didn't know what to think. There seemed to be limited possibilities. One, I *did* have hyperactive glands and was, maybe, nuts. Two, Nate had underactive glands, or was, maybe, another late bloomer.

I was just too curious to worry about turning Nate off girls for life. I really wanted to know if he had any of the same weird impulses toward G. G. that I had toward Darlene. I was almost as curious about how G. G. kissed him as I was about how he kissed G. G.

"Does she like it when you kiss her on the neck?" I asked, talking real fast. "It makes Darlene crazy," I lied. Well, I was sure it would, if I could ever get to her neck.

"Whoo, aren't we getting a little too up-close and personal, Horrible Hobe?"

"Aw, come on, Nate. You can tell me. We've been friends for years. Girls talk about this stuff all the time."

"Look, Hobe, we kiss when we feel like it. She likes it, I like it. I can't give you a play-by-play description. G. G. isn't a hockey game; she's a girl."

"So she's got you fooled too?" I muttered. I was beginning to feel frustrated.

"Hobe." Nate's tone was mild, but there was a definite note of warning in it. "We're still friends. You can ask me anything you want, except for personal questions about G. G. And you can say anything you want—except nasty things about her."

"That sort of cuts down on the conversational possibilities, doesn't it?"

"You could tell me about you and Darlene."

Was he kidding? After he'd been so close-mouthed about G. G.? Even though I'd been burning to talk to him about Darlene, I sure wasn't going to now.

"What's to tell?" I shrugged. "You've got eyes in your head, right?"

"That's the only reason you like her? Because of how she looks?"

"There's a better reason?" I said sarcastically.

Maybe there was a better reason, and maybe I'd think of it later, but when Darlene came into the bookstore at three-thirty, the way she looked was all the reasons I needed.

This time she practically dragged *me* into the back room—I thought my grandfather was going to pop an artery trying to keep from laughing.

The moment we were through the door she grabbed me around the neck and pulled my head down. She was in such a hurry to kiss me that our front teeth bumped. She wasn't kidding when she said she couldn't wait to see me! When she let me go I staggered back against the metal shelves. Holy cow—what had I done to this innocent child? She'd turned into a wild woman.

"Where's the poem?"

It had been a mistake, I realized now, to ever rouse Darlene's latent literary appetites. The fastest pen in the east couldn't satisfy her colossal craving for rhyme. The girl had become a poetry junkie. And I was her supplier.

"The poem's in my notebook. I left it up front."

"Go get it. I'm dying to see it."

I went back to the counter to get my notebook. I avoided my grandfather's eye. I probably had lipstick all over my face. I thought I heard him stifle a giggle.

Darlene practically snatched the poem out of my hands and devoured it in one gulp, her lips racing over the syllables as her eyes scanned the lines.

"Oh, Hobie, it's fantastic! It's *perfect*. I think it's the best one you ever wrote! Will you write me another one?"

"Good grief, Darlene, you haven't even digested this one yet! Gimme a break, will you? I'm not made of ink, you know. Now come here and show me how mush you miched me."

Good Lord, my nerves were shot. The strain of trying to keep up with Darlene's epic demands while cruelly deprived of the inspiration only she could provide had finally gotten to me. No wonder so many writers drank. This creative life was *murder*.

I guess Darlene finally figured out that what I'd been trying to say before I cracked was, "Come here and show me how much you missed me," because she wound her suede-covered arms around my neck—she was *never* going to take off that jacket—and began kissing my face again.

"Dear Hobie," she murmured. "Sweet Hobie." She sounded almost like she was soothing a little baby. But she started running her fingers through my hair, which wasn't soothing at all, and said, "When I can't see you I read the poems and think of you . . . that's why they're so important to me. . . . So will you write me another one?"

What could I say? Knowing that my poems were the only way she could stand our separations, imagining her reading them, kissing them, holding them to her heart, how could I complain about writer's block?

Plus, Darlene was messing up my hair as completely as she'd messed up my head, twining her fingers in it and rumpling it till my hair felt like it was *alive*.

If ever anyone had mastered the seduction secrets of the black widow spider, it was Darlene. If ever a fly had been trapped by a champion web weaver, it was me.

"I'll try," I whimpered, as she trailed one delicate finger down the back of my neck. "But Darlene . . . *darling* . . . maybe, once in a while . . . I mean, if I get stuck . . . couldn't you reread one?"

I almost pressed fifty-five pounds that evening. My father was really excited about it.

"It won't be long now, Hobie old boy! Maybe a week."

I wasn't sure I'd last a week.

I found myself standing behind Shawna Shepherd and Lesley Parker on the lunch line the next day. I was thinking about Darlene's delicate, pink-tipped fingers running roughshod through my hair, and Darlene's lips like moist fruit murmuring in my ear, and generally trying to inspire myself to write another poem by tomorrow afternoon. So I wasn't paying too much attention to their whispering and giggling. Not at first.

The cafeteria aide ladled out some chow mein. I put the dish on my tray, and slid the tray down the metal rails toward the fruit salad.

". . . never know it to look at him," Lesley was saying. "I mean, that last one, about without you my life is death, that's really *deep*."

Suddenly, I paid very close attention. Darlene had told them! She'd shown Lesley and Shawna my poems. She couldn't resist—she was too overcome by our love to keep it a secret. She must have made them promise not to tell anyone else. I hoped they didn't notice that I was right behind them. I wanted to hear more about how profound and talented everyone thought I was. Even though you wouldn't know it to look at me.

"And they're really good. That's what's so surprising. You don't expect a jock to be writing love poems at all, let alone . . ."

A jock? I wasn't a jock. Sure, I was doing pretty well with the weights, but I didn't think anyone knew about that.

"Shh! There he is!" I smiled modestly as they giggled and shushed each other. They must have just realized that I was standing behind them.

Lesley fumbled in her wallet as they reached the cashier and Shawna said, "Be quiet! And stop staring at him! She'll kill us if anyone finds out."

Staring? But Lesley wasn't staring at me. In fact, she wasn't looking at me at all. She'd been peering all the way toward the back of the line.

This was very strange. I turned around to see who they were talking about—even though it had to be me. Warren Adler stood at the end of the line, with a tray under each arm, waiting his turn at the chow mein.

Warren Adler. A jock. A certified jock, with the letter to prove it. But not a poet. *I* was the poet. There couldn't be any mistake about that, because Lesley had even quoted one of my lines.

I must have just stood there awhile because I heard the guy behind me say, "Hey, come on, move it." I don't know how much money I gave the cashier. She dumped some change on my tray and said, "Go on, go on, move along."

The lunchroom was a blur. I found a table and sat down, but everything was foggy.

"You don't expect a jock to write love poems," Shawna had said. And then, "There he is!" Looking right past me, at Warren.

And then, in a flash, it was all gruesomely clear.

Darlene was showing her friends my poems and telling them that Warren had given them to her.

My gut felt like a block of ice.

It explained everything. All the suspicious things Darlene had said and done, the "wrong" feeling I couldn't shake no matter how much Darlene kissed me.

No wonder we had to keep our "love" a secret. Not because of her mother. Darlene didn't want anyone to see us going out together, or to see me giving her the poems, because she wanted them to think it was Warren who was hopelessly in love with her.

Warren, who she still had a crush on after all, who she probably kept on chasing the whole time she pretended to love me.

She'd used me. She'd made a fool of me. All her kisses, all her words, *lies!* The whole thing was an act, just to get me to write the poems. She'd probably dreamed up the idea the day I gave her the first one, the one G. G. had picked up from the library floor.

I stared miserably into my chow mein.

Why? *Why,* Darlene? I loved you. Your lips like moist fruit, your hair like new-mown wheat . . .

Warren doesn't love you. What can you get out of pretending he does?

Again I remembered what Jennifer had said about the kind of person who uses someone else to build himself up. Could Darlene use me like this, just for a game of Let's Pretend? Could she kiss me without really liking me when she knew how much I cared about her?

I mean, it wasn't like this would get Warren to pay attention to her; she told her friends to keep it a secret not only because of me, but so that Warren wouldn't find out what she was up to. It was just a *game*. Darlene was showing off, trying to look big to her friends.

I couldn't understand it. I'd offered Darlene true love and heartfelt poetry, and all she ever really wanted was broad shoulders and overdeveloped muscles.

How shallow can you be?

I tried to tell myself it was just as well that I found out Darlene's true character now, so I wouldn't waste any more time and emotion on a girl so unworthy, so treacherous, so *immature;* a girl so purely concerned with the physical instead of the spiritual.

But I couldn't help wondering, what if I hadn't found out how selfish and deceitful Darlene was? What if she'd just gone on inspiring me and running her fingers through my hair? What if I'd just gone on writing her poems and receiving her kisses?

I could think of worse ways to spend my life.

* * *

I pressed fifty-five pounds that night. Darlene was my inspiration. I only had to remember her phoney "secret smile" as I'd walked past her desk that afternoon, and I gave out a mighty roar and hoisted the barbell over my head.

My father cheered and clapped as I staggered for a few seconds, then lowered the weights to the floor. "Great going! You'll be doing sixty before you know it."

"I don't think so." I started up the stairs. "I'm beginning to think that muscles are vastly over-rated."

I went to my room. There was one last poem I had to write to Darlene.

And I couldn't wait to see her face when she read it.

The next afternoon I stopped at Darlene's desk and handed her the poem.

"Not here," she whispered. "Later."

"There is no later, baby," I snarled. "Read it."

She was very flustered. She didn't know what was going on, but whatever it was, she didn't want anyone to see it going on. Finally she looked down at the sheet of paper.

I watched her lips form the words. I watched her eyes grow wide till they practically bugged out of her head. I think the signature was the killer.

She gawked at me. She struggled to say something, I guess to try and pretend she didn't know what this was all about. But she wasn't going to be able to pretend with me anymore. Or with anyone else.

"Show this one to your friends, sweetheart." I knew she wouldn't. She'd never show this little gem to anyone.

My final, heartfelt, sincerely inspired poem to Darlene read:

> *Violets are blue,*
> *Roses are red,*
> *Get off my case,*
>   *Or I'll slam-dunk your head.*

I'd signed it "Warren."

✺ 15 ✺

Your hair is like a sunset,
And your eyes are emerald seas,
And when I see the ocean,
I will always think of ~~these.~~ ~~thee.~~ ~~these.~~
thee.

Terrible.

Let me swim in the emerald pools of your eyes—

Bleachh. Disgusting.

Your hair is flame, your eyes green ice—

AND I THINK YOU'RE VERY NICE. LET ME KISS YOU
once or twice. I like chicken soup with rice.

I'll work on it.

Every once in a while I still have a disturbing
thought about Darlene and her hair and her lips and

her general lusciousness, but I know now that I made an epic mistake in spurning G. G.'s deep and sincere affection. Darlene was merely a physical attraction. There isn't a whole lot to Darlene except scheming and plotting. In fact, I was probably as guilty as she was of being shallow and physical instead of sincere and spiritual.

But G. G. There's a girl who *really* inspires me.

G. G. has it all—brains, sympathy, maturity, niceness, honesty, hair like a sunset, eyes like emeralds. . . .

Of course, technically she's still going with Nate, and naturally I don't want to do anything that would hurt my best friend, but to tell you the truth, I don't think Nate's all that wrapped up in G. G. I mean, not like I am.

They don't even hold hands very often. Which is just as well, because when they do my stomach feels like it was stabbed in the heart. I don't think Nate appreciates the subtle nuances of handholding.

Frankly, I think the whole thing is more like a friendship than a romance. I think pretty soon G. G. will come to realize that she's never gotten over me, any more than Darlene got over Warren Adler. Nate probably won't mind that much, especially now that spring training is about to start down in Florida.

So I figure it's only a matter of time till Nate and G. G. drift apart. And just a matter of time till I write the perfect poem.

(The last time my father asked me what I planned to do with my life I told him I was thinking about becoming a poet. He turned purple. He hasn't asked me another question about my "goals" since then. I guess he doesn't want to hear the answer. So that worked out okay.)

Anyway, when I write the perfect poem, G. G. will read it, press it to her heart and look up at me with those gorgeous emerald eyes. "Oh, Hobie," she'll say, "I've waited so long for this moment."

It has to work out that way. It just *has* to.

Because every time I see her, every time she smiles at me, every time I think about her—even about how her killer perfume nearly wasted me in the library that fateful day—my brain gets dreamy and stupid and I can't concentrate on anything. Not even the new Mac Detroit book, *Blood before Breakfast*.

I can't think about anyone but G. G.

That girl is driving me *crazy*.

**Fast-paced, action-packed stories—
the ultimate adventure/mystery series!**

COMING SOON . . .
HAVE YOU SEEN
THE HARDY BOYS LATELY?

Beginning in April 1987, all-new Hardy Boys mysteries will be available in pocket-sized editions called THE HARDY BOYS CASEFILES.

Frank and Joe Hardy are eighties guys with eighties interests, living in Bayport, U.S.A. Their extracurricular activities include girlfriends, fast-food joints, hanging out at the mall and quad theaters. But computer whiz Frank and the charming, athletic Joe are deep into international intrigue and high-tech drama. The pace of these mysteries just never lets up!

For a sample of the *new* Hardy Boys, turn the page and enjoy excerpts from DEAD ON TARGET and EVIL, INC., the first two books in THE HARDY BOYS CASEFILES.

And don't forget to look for more of the new Hardy Boys and details about a great Hardy Boys contest in April!

THE HARDY BOYS CASEFILES™

Case #1
Dead on Target

**A terrorist bombing sends Frank and Joe
on a mission of revenge.**

"GET OUT OF my way, Frank!" Joe Hardy shoved past his brother, shouting to be heard over the roar of the flames. Straight ahead, a huge fireball rose like a mushroom cloud over the parking lot. Flames shot fifty feet into the air, dropping chunks of wreckage—wreckage that just a moment earlier had been their yellow sedan. "Iola's in there! We've got to get her out!"

Frank stared, his lean face frozen in shock, as his younger brother ran straight for the billowing flames. Then he raced after Joe, catching him in a flying tackle twenty feet away from the blaze. Even at that distance they could feel the heat.

"Do you want to get yourself killed?" Frank yelled, rising to his knees.

Joe remained silent, his blue eyes staring at the wall of flame, his blond hair mussed by the fall.

Frank hauled his brother around, making Joe face him. "She wouldn't have lasted a second," he said, trying to soften the blow. "Face it, Joe."

For an instant, Frank thought the message had gotten through. Joe sagged against the concrete. Then he surged up again, eyes wild. "No! I can save her! Let go!"

Before Joe could get to his feet, Frank tackled him again, sending both of them tumbling along the ground. Joe began struggling, thrashing against his brother's grip. With near-maniacal strength, he broke Frank's hold, then started throwing wild punches at his brother, almost as if he were grateful to have a physical enemy to attack.

Frank blocked the flailing blows, lunging forward to grab Joe again. But a fist pounded through his guard, catching him full in the mouth. Frank flopped on his back, stunned, as his brother lurched to his feet and staggered toward the inferno.

Painfully pulling himself up, Frank wiped something wet from his lips—blood. He sprinted after Joe, blindly snatching at his T-shirt. The fabric tore loose in his hand.

Forcing himself farther into the glare and suffocating heat, Frank managed to get a grip on his brother's arm. Joe didn't even try to shake free. He just pulled both of them closer to the flames.

The air was so hot it scorched Frank's throat as he gasped for breath. He flipped Joe free, throwing him off balance. Then he wrapped one arm around Joe's neck and cocked the other back, flashing in a karate blow. Joe went limp in his brother's arms.

As Frank dragged them both out of danger, he heard the wail of sirens in the distance. We should never have come, he thought, never.

Just an hour before, Joe had jammed the brakes on the car, stopping in front of the mall. "So *this* is why we had to come here," he exclaimed. "They're having a rally! Give me a break, Iola."

"You knew we were working on the campaign." Iola grinned, looking like a little dark-haired pixie. "Would you have come if we'd told you?"

"No way! What do you think, we're going to stand around handing out Walker for President buttons?" Joe scowled at his girlfriend.

"Actually, they're leaflets," Callie Shaw said from the backseat. She leaned forward to peer at herself in the rearview mirror and ran her fingers hastily through her short brown hair.

"So that's what you've got stuck between us!" Frank rapped the cardboard box on the seat.

"I thought you liked Walker," said Callie.

"He's all right," Frank admitted. "He looked good on TV last night, saying we should fight back against terrorists. At least he's not a wimp."

"That antiterrorism thing has gotten a lot of coverage," Iola said. "Besides . . ."

". . . He's cute," Frank cut in, mimicking Iola.

"The most gorgeous politician I've ever seen."

Laughter cleared the air as they pulled into a parking space. "Look, we're not really into passing out pamphlets—or leaflets, or whatever they are," Frank said. "But we will do something to help. We'll beef up your crowd."

"Yeah," Joe grumbled. "It sounds like a real hot afternoon."

The mall was a favorite hangout for Bayport kids—three floors with more than a hundred stores arranged around a huge central well. The Saturday sunshine streamed down from the glass roof to ground level—the Food Floor. But that day, instead of the usual tables for pizzas, burgers, and burritos, the space had been cleared out, except for a band, which was tuning up noisily.

The music blasted up to the roof, echoing in the huge open space. Heads began appearing, staring down, along the safety railings that lined the shopping levels. Still more shoppers gathered on the Food Floor. Callie, Iola, and four other kids circulated through the crowd, handing out leaflets.

The Food Floor was packed with people cheering and applauding. But Frank Hardy backed away, turned off by all the hype. Since he'd lost Joe after about five seconds in the jostling mob, he fought his way to the edges of the crowd, trying to spot him.

Joe was leaning against one of the many pillars supporting the mall. He had a big grin on his face and was talking with a gorgeous blond girl. Frank hurried over to them. But Joe, deep in conversation with his new friend, didn't notice his brother. More importantly, he didn't notice his girlfriend making her way through the crowd.

Frank arrived about two steps behind Iola, who had wrapped one arm around Joe's waist while glaring at the blond. "Oh, uh, hi," said Joe, his grin fading in embarrassment. "This is Val. She just came—"

"I'd love to stay and talk," Iola said, cutting Joe off, "but we have a problem. We're running out of leaflets. The only ones left are on the backseat of your car. Could you help me get them?"

"Right now? We just got here," Joe complained.

"Yeah, and I can see you're really busy," Iola said, looking at Val. "Are you coming?"

Joe hesitated for a moment, looking from Iola to the blond girl. "Okay." His hand fished around in his pocket and came out with his car keys. "I'll be with you in a minute, okay?" He started playing catch with the keys, tossing them in the air as he turned back to Val.

But Iola angrily snatched the keys in midair. Then she rushed off, nearly knocking Frank over.

"Hey, Joe, I've got to talk to you," Frank said, smiling at Val as he took his brother by the elbow. "Excuse us a second." He pulled Joe around the pillar.

"What's going on?" Joe complained. "I can't even start a friendly conversation without everybody jumping on me."

"You know, it's lucky you're so good at picking up girls," said Frank. "Because you sure are tough on the ones you already know."

Joe's face went red. "What are you talking about?"

"You know what I'm talking about. I saw your little trick with the keys there a minute ago. You made Iola look like a real jerk in front of some girl you've been hitting on. Make up your mind, Joe. Is Iola your girlfriend or not?"

Joe seemed to be studying the toes of his running shoes as Frank spoke. "You're right, I guess," he finally muttered. "But I was gonna go! Why did she have to make such a life-and-death deal out of it?"

Frank grinned. "It's your fatal charm, Joe. It stirs up women's passions."

"Very funny." Joe sighed. "So what should I do?"

"Let's go out to the car and give Iola a hand," Frank suggested. "She can't handle that big box all by herself."

He put his head around the pillar and smiled at Val. "Sorry. I have to borrow this guy for a while. We'll be back in a few minutes."

They headed for the nearest exit. The sleek, modern mall decor gave way to painted cinderblocks as they headed down the corridor to the underground parking garages. "We should've caught up to her by now," Joe said as they came to the first row of cars. "She must be really steamed."

He was glancing around for Iola, but the underground lot was a perfect place for hide-and-seek. Every ten feet or so, squat concrete pillars which supported the upper levels rose from the floor, blocking the view. But as the Hardys reached the end of the row of cars, they saw a dark-haired figure marching angrily ahead of them.

"Iola!" Joe called.

Instead of turning around, Iola put on speed.

"Hey, Iola, wait a minute!" Joe picked up his pace, but Iola darted around a pillar. A second later she'd disappeared.

"Calm down," Frank said. "She'll be outside at the car. You can talk to her then."

Joe led the way to the outdoor parking lot, nervously pacing ahead of Frank. "She's really angry," he said as they stepped outside. "I just hope she doesn't—"

The explosion drowned out whatever he was going to say. They ran to the spot where they'd parked their yellow sedan. But the car—and Iola—had erupted in a ball of white-hot flame!

Case #2
Evil, Inc.

When Frank and Joe take on Reynard and Company, they find that murder is business as usual.

THE FRENCH POLICE officer kept his eyes on the two teenagers from the moment they sat down at the outdoor café across the street from the Pompidou Center in Paris.

Those two kids spelled trouble. The cop knew their type. *Les punks* was what the French called them. Both of them had spiky hair; one had dyed his jet black, the other bright green. They wore identical black T-shirts emblazoned with the words *The Poison Pens* in brilliant yellow, doubtless some unpleasant rock group. Their battered, skintight black trousers seemed ready to split at the seams. And their scuffed black leather combat boots looked as if they had gone through a couple of wars. A gold earring gleamed on one earlobe of each boy.

What were they waiting for? the cop wondered. Somebody to mug? Somebody to sell drugs to? He was sure of one thing: the punks were up to no good as they sat waiting and watchful at their table, nursing tiny cups of black coffee. True, one of them looked very interested in any pretty girl who passed by. But when a couple of girls stopped in front of the table, willing to be friendly, the second punk said something sharp to the first, who shrugged a silent apology to the girls. The girls shrugged back and went on their way, leaving the two punks to scan the passing crowd.

The cop wished he could hear their conversation and find out what language they spoke. You couldn't tell kids' nationalities nowadays by their appearance. Teen styles crossed all boundaries, he had decided.

If the cop had been able to hear the two boys, he would have known instantly where they were from.

"Cool it. This is no time to play Casanova," one of them said.

"Aw, come on," the other answered. "So many girls—so little time."

Their voices were as American as apple pie, even if their appearances weren't.

In fact, their voices were the only things about them that even their closest friends back home would have recognized.

"Let's keep our minds on the job," Frank Hardy told his brother.

"Remember what they say about all work and no play," Joe Hardy answered.

"And *you* remember that if we make one wrong move here in Paris," Frank said, "it'll be our last."

Sitting in the summer late-afternoon sunlight at the Café des Nations, Frank was having a hard time keeping Joe's mind on business. He had no sooner made Joe break off a budding friendship with two pretty girls who had stopped in front of their table, when another one appeared. One look at her, and Frank knew that Joe would be hard to discourage.

She looked about eighteen years old. Her pale complexion was flawless and untouched by makeup except for dark shading around her green eyes. Her hair was flaming red, and if it was dyed, it was very well done. She wore a white T-shirt that showed off her slim figure, faded blue jeans that hugged her legs down to her bare ankles, and high-heeled sandals. Joe didn't have to utter a word to say what he thought of her. His eyes said it all: Gorgeous!

Even Frank wasn't exactly eager to get rid of her.

Especially when she leaned toward them, gave them a smile, and said, "Brother, can you spare a million?"

"Sit down," Joe said instantly.

But the girl remained standing. Her gaze flicked toward the policeman who stood watching them.

"Too hot out here in the sun," she said with the faintest of French accents. "I know someplace that's cooler. Come on."

Frank left some change on the table to pay for the coffees, then he and Joe hurried off with the girl.

"What's your name?" Joe asked.

"Denise," she replied. "And which brother are you, Joe or Frank?"

"I'm Joe," Joe said. "The handsome, charming one."

"Where are we going?" asked Frank.

"And that's Frank," Joe added. "The dull, businesslike one."

"Speaking of business," said Denise, "do you have the money?"

"Do you have the goods?" asked Frank.

"*Trust* the young lady," Joe said, putting his arm around her shoulder. "Anyone who looks as good as she does can't be bad."

"First, you answer," Denise said to Frank.

"I've got the money," said Frank.

"Then I've got the goods," said Denise.

The Hardys and Denise were walking through a maze of twisting streets behind the Pompidou Center. Denise glanced over her shoulder each time they turned, making sure they weren't being followed. Finally she seemed satisfied.

"In here," she said, indicating the entranceway to a grime-covered old building.

They entered a dark hallway, and Denise flicked a switch.

"We have to hurry up the stairs," she said. "The light stays on for just sixty seconds."

At the top of the creaking stairs was a steel door, which clearly had been installed to discourage thieves. Denise rapped loudly on it: four raps, a pause, and then two more.

The Hardys heard the sound of a bolt being unfastened and then a voice saying, *"Entrez."*

Denise swung the door open and motioned for Frank and Joe to go in first.

They did.

A man was waiting for them in the center of a shabbily furnished room.

Neither Frank nor Joe could have said what he looked like.

All they could see was what was in his hand.

It was a pistol—and it was pointed directly at them.

**And don't miss these other
exciting all-new adventures in
THE HARDY BOYS CASEFILES**

Case #3
Cult of Crime

High in the untamed Adirondack Mountains lurks one of
the most fiendish plots Frank and Joe Hardy have ever
encountered. On a mission to rescue their good friend
Holly from the cult of the lunatic Rajah, the boys unwit-
tingly become the main event in one of the madman's
deadly rituals—human sacrifice.

Fleeing from gun-wielding "religious" zealots and riding
a danger-infested train through the wilderness, Frank and
Joe arrive home to find the worst has happened. The Rajah
and his followers have invaded Bayport. As their
hometown is about to go up in flames, the boys look to
Holly for help. But Holly has plans of her own, and one
deadly secret.

Available in May 1987.

Case #4
The Lazarus Plot

Camped out in the Maine woods, the Hardy boys get a real jolt when they glimpse Joe's old girlfriend, Iola Morton. Can it really be the same girl who was blown to bits before their eyes by a terrorist bomb? Frantically searching for her, Frank and Joe are trapped in the lair of the most diabolical team of scientists ever assembled.

Twisting technology to their own ends, the criminals create perfect replicas of the boys. Now the survival of a top-secret government intelligence organization is at stake. Frank and Joe must discover the bizarre truth about Iola and face their doubles alone—before the scientists unleash one final, deadly experiment.

Available in June 1987.

HAVE YOU SEEN
NANCY
DREW®
LATELY?

Nancy Drew has become a girl of the 80's! There is
hardly a girl from seven to seventeen who doesn't
know her name.

Now you can continue to enjoy Nancy Drew in a new
series, written for older readers–THE NANCY DREW®
FILES. Each pocket-sized book has more romance,
fashion, mystery and adventure.

In THE NANCY DREW® FILES, Nancy pursues one
thrilling adventure after another. With her boundless
energy and intelligence, Nancy finds herself investi-
gating a crime-ridden high school, vacationing in Fort
Lauderdale with her friends Bess and George, intern-
ing at a New York based teen magazine, and going to
rock concerts.

THE NANCY DREW® FILES

#1 SECRETS CAN KILL
#2 DEADLY INTENT
#3 MURDER ON ICE
#4 SMILE AND SAY MURDER
#5 HIT-AND-RUN HOLIDAY
#6 WHITE WATER TERROR
#7 DEADLY DOUBLES
#8 TWO POINTS
   FOR MURDER

Archway Paperbacks
Published by Pocket Books
A Division of Simon & Schuster, Inc.   527